PACIFIC

By Trevor J. Houser

Portions of this work first appeared, in slightly different form, in Zyzzyva (Spring 2007) and Flock (April 2017).

Attention schools and businesses: for discounted copies on large orders, please contact the publisher directly. Retailers and libraries can order copies through Ingram

Unsolicited Press
Portland, Oregon
www.unsolicitedpress.com
info@unsolicitedpress.com
619-354-8005

Author Photo: Andrew Wicklund
Cover Design: Andy Babbitz
Editor: Kay Grey
ISBN: 978-1-950730-84-1

For Lizzy and Colonel Artichoke

And for my wife

PACIFIC

The sea is everything.

Jules Verne

THE PACIFIC OCEAN

THE PACIFIC OCEAN is the largest and deepest of the Earth's waterbodies. It is 165.25 million square kilometers in total area, including rusty battleships, Prussian blue, and Amelia Earhart.

If you were in space, it's the main thing you would see.

You would feel the massiveness of it.

You would feel the sharks and the old starfish sinking down into your throat. From the thermosphere to the Sea of Nectar, you would feel it. The view would be quite impressive.

The Mariana Trench is down there.

My father's Budweiser bottle from 1984 is down there.

It looks the way you would like an ocean to look. Both inviting and intimidating.

When the three of us first saw the ocean together he was 10 weeks old and my future ex-wife and I knew nothing about arteriovenous malformations or divorce settlements. It was a cold, bright afternoon and we brought sandwiches and beer to sit with and watch the waves from our car, a churning blue-green.

The Pacific is where we are now.

On the Tiffany I, which is actually the old Anna Marie II. Just me and my son and the captain who likes doing blow off the echo sounder. Recurring drug-problem or no, he's my oldest friend and knows his way around a ship. He is taking us to Guatemala to see a doctor for my son's brain, which for some reason is trying to kill him. He is almost five and has eyes like the bottom of a swimming pool. Somewhere I have whisky and my Beretta. He has Captain America and my green Hot Wheels Jaguar XJS circa 1978.

PART ONE

CAPTAIN AMERICA WAS HERE

I HAVE A family. In the gray island-mists north of Seattle I have them. We bought a house in a place called Wolf Island with big Asian maples overlooking Padilla Bay. That first spring I drank wine on the porch and felt so proud. Sunlight through the mist and mossy trees. Feeling like life made sense. Do you know that feeling?

Except now we have a child who might die.

No one is sure. So many children die. But this is our child, so it's different.

He has a rare brain disease. Like so rare if you say it in most hospitals they look at you with eyes that are kind but vacant, like a trout's eyes as you lower it back into a cold spring stream.

Now I sit on street corners. I sit there and look at mountains or apartment buildings between me and the mountains. I sit there and look at cars and houses and lawnmowers with icicles on them.

Once we spoke to the doctors and they laughed. We all tried to laugh. We all tried to make it like it was something we could control. It was something humans had power over like the stock market or electronica. It was something that didn't make you want to go back in time to when the world was saturated and beautiful and untouched. That was a different person. That was a person putting a little blue sweater on this boy. He hated hats. He hated putting on shoes. He hated so many things.

Now we go to the doctor and laugh.

He looks at nurses and makes jokes and runs up and down the halls and they laugh. Bells. Stars. Planets go by. He is underneath all of that and he shows God what it means. God probably looks down. God looks down, I'm sure. God watches him and his rare diseased brain that is so rare and diseased his pediatrician had never heard of it.

One afternoon, I cried over the sink while eating an avocado.

It was an old avocado that I ate still in its cling wrap as more clouds formed above our small, lumpy yard. I was eating the avocado and looking out at our yard, the mysterious lumps, the sky, the trees. I just sort of smooshed half the avocado into my mouth, thinking of my son. His brain has blood vessels that are too large. His small heart. His small heart is so small.

I could become important. I could drive a speedboat over an iceberg with the Dave Matthews Band playing on the prow and nothing would change. I could become a Navy Seal, the best ever, and his brain would still have too much blood inside it. Those vessels would become enlarged. His eyes would widen as we watch some muted game show on the TV that's bolted to the wall surrounded by other children facing the possibility of death. His brain would expand. Or it already has.

On Sundays, we play Captain America.

He has the pajamas with the stars and stripes. He runs so fast and jumps nearly over the bed. He runs and jumps on the bed and makes this noise that isn't a scream but has the same energy of a scream.

He makes noise.

He jumps and laughs.

GO BETWEEN THE MOON AND THE MILKMAN

ONE DAY I take out our old lawnmower while still in uniform, and I mow our lawn. Then I mow the grass on the sidewalk. Then I keep mowing. I mow across the street. I watch the neighbors watching me mow across the street. I keep mowing. I mow the next block. I take the mower across the busy intersection and begin mowing the grass in a different neighborhood. I know they are looking at me. I know they know I'm not the right person to be mowing their lawns. The Wolf Island chief of police mowing random peoples' lawns just doesn't look right.

Did I mention I'm the police chief?

It doesn't matter.

I just watch their grass filing down shorter and shorter into my little burlap bag and take out an old pack of cigarettes and light one up. I smoke the cigarette and look up at the daytime moon, all white and faded like an old hospital gown. My son always points it out with excitement. *The moon's right there! Just above!* I never really thought about it. Not until he came along and started pointing it out all the time. I'd always just noticed the moon at night, but now I try to notice it more.

"Oh, hey chief," someone says tentatively from their driveway.

"Hey!" I say, and then I get back to mowing.

DRIVING BLIND

AFTER MY SON'S last surgery, we thought he'd gone blind. "A complication," said the doctors. Anyway, he couldn't see so I handed him a Hot Wheels car and we both played Hot Wheels on his hospital bed, using the creases and folds like jumping ramps. He kept blinking and trying to see and making the sounds of a car jumping over massive canyons of stiff blue cotton that said, "St. Luke's." My wife was crying, piled up somewhere near the air conditioner. I think maybe there was a nurse. It was nighttime outside in New York City. The window was cracked to let in the fresh air. You could hear taxi cabs and a bar playing jazz somewhere. It was late summer. My son had suction cups and wires sticking out all over him like a billboard for death. He probably wasn't even the sickest person in this hospital, I thought, as we jumped our cars from one of his little knees to mine. Other children might've actually died in there that day. Their tiny hearts and lungs failed somewhere windowless and cold, and never got to play Hot Wheels one last time with their father, hearing faraway jazz on a summer evening.

After a couple hours, my son began to regain his eyesight, but I remember thinking at the time he might be blind for life. He just kept playing cars, though, so I did, too.

He reminds me of myself in a lot of ways, although I come from a heart diseased people.

In the winter of 1980, my grandfather died of a heart attack and I ran away from home with three cans of tomato soup. I lived in a thatch of bamboo in the neighbor's yard. A few hours later my parents found me and took me home. They fed me some of the tomato soup with saltine crackers and a chocolate square for dessert.

"How do you feel now?" they asked.

"Good," I lied, feeling hollow, and thinking about death more than ever.

As my father got ready for work the next morning, I alerted him to the presence of a six-foot albino witch who, at the time, I was certain lived on a branch outside my bedroom window.

"She wants to pull my guts out," I told him.

"Oh yeah," my father said, shaving in his black socks and tighty-whities. "What's the old gal's name?"

"I don't know," I said, "but I think she wants to eat my guts while I'm still alive."

"It's alright kiddo." He patted my head. "No more scary movies for awhile, ok?"

He went back to shaving. He owned a private security company and years later also died of heart failure while looking at magazines in the Denver airport.

While he shaved, I went inside a closet behind some old smelly coats and cried. I was crying because one day my father would be in the ground with grandpa, and the albino witch would be eating my guts while I was still alive. Once I even tried talking to grandpa through the floor heater, but he couldn't hear me because of all the dirt in his ears. Then I got older and worried more about the imperviousness of bra straps which begat mortgages which begat interventional radiologists on 99th and Madison.

I didn't have time for six-foot albino witches and speaking to the dead.

STARLIGHT EXPRESS

THERE IS NOTHING special about me. I realized this in my twenty-ninth year, somewhere between Olympia and Vancouver aboard the Starlight Express, which sounds a lot better than it is. It was like a thunderclap of dull light piercing the deep, dark evening. Probably teeming with others of my generation who had somehow dodged mediocrity. They had secured better jobs. More thrilling sex lives. More Swedish-made automobiles with titanium alloy in places my patrol jeep had lint and/or a yellow coffee mug with Wonder Woman on it.

I had been visiting my old high school friend who now does coke and fish for a living, but this was before all the fish and immediately following his botched and coke-fueled engagement. After a weekend of drunken moral support, I was California-bound and nursing a Finlandia on the rocks. I was drinking it while admiring the cheap leather and Velcro that belonged to me for twenty-two and a half hours along the northwest corridor down to San Francisco for $76.89. I remember looking out at the dusky marshland and the old gas stations lit up like rusty Christmas trees. What is my purpose here, I thought? I had no cause. Unless you counted Hungarian nurse porn, or not having to shoot people in the line of duty. I also liked semi-soft cheeses and promotional calendars from the 50s. Maybe instead of being a cop I should get into wine importing, I thought. Or go on a church mission to teach Peruvians how to shoot contested step-back threes. Who knows? Maybe there's a trajectory of failed dreams you can see from outer space. It looks like a storm system, or a lost continent. You see it in a satellite photo while sitting in your favorite chair, drinking a martini that could wipeout an anthill. You cry a little looking at the satellite photo. You look out the window. You watch a repeat of Iron Chef. You go to bed thinking, tomorrow—tomorrow will be a little better somehow.

TEN YEARS LATER

I MET MY wife and bought our first flat screen TV and had a child and moved from San Francisco to become police chief of Wolf Island and our son was diagnosed with Vein of Galen Malformation as my wife and I sunk into the floorboards while discussing "possibilities" with a doctor on the phone, frozen enchiladas aflame in the oven.

THE INCIDENT

MY WIFE WANTS to talk about the "lawn-mowing incident."

"What do you mean, 'incident?'" I say, pouring another Old Fitz.

"This...well, I got a call from lots of different people about this mowing everyone's lawn or whatever."

I take a long sip from my drink and sit back down in my chair that faces a window looking out on the big Asian maples, bending in the wind.

"It's nothing," I say. "I just started mowing our lawn and thought, you know, why not just mow the whole neighborhood."

"And a few other neighborhoods?"

"Yeah, maybe," I say, thinking how much I wanted to love her. "You want to watch a movie tonight or something? Or maybe I could go get some steaks and grill them before the storm picks up."

She looks out the window, at the bending maples, which is a thing she does more and more these days, usually accompanied by a sigh or an eye roll.

"We need to talk," she says, taking the kind of breath you take before lowering yourself into a cryogenics capsule. "I don't want any more surgeries for him. Like the doctor said, maybe in a couple years the blood vessels could get bigger and we might have a chance…"

"What about the doctor in Guatemala or wherever?"

"The fucking witch-doctor?"

"He's Austrian. There are no witch doctors named Haas."

"Why isn't he in Austria then?"

"Because it's experimental. It's fucking cutting edge. Jesus. You know why."

"Exactly. And you're willing to put him at risk like that again?"

"He's already at risk, honey. You heard the doctor. Did you hear him? He could…if we don't do anything…"

"And he definitely will die a lot quicker if we…goddamn…fuck it!"

Then she goes out to "get some air" and the house is quiet again.

Just me and the bending Asian maples and Old Fitz and my son somewhere playing Hot Wheels, thinking of nothing.

ARMOR

ONE DAY WE were playing nerf basketball in his room and he asked me why he was always going to the hospital.

"We just need to make you better," I told him.

"Is something wrong with me?" he said.

"You have this thing that needs special attention is all."

"Why do some kids not have to go to the hospital?"

"Lots of kids have to go."

"Not Caleb, or Lily, or Felix."

"No, not them," I say, imagining Felix's parents walking by a children's hospital, holding hands, laughing, making paper airplanes out of someone's old test results.

"Why don't they go?" he says.

"Well, they're just not as strong as you," I say. "You have to be a strong, big boy to go to the hospital."

He considers this for a moment, slowly turning the small basketball over in his hands. He's remembering the smells. He's remembering the faint noises the machines make all through the night like lost fishing trawlers.

"Sometimes I'm kind of a little scared," he says, not looking up.

"That's ok, kiddo," I say. "That's totally normal. But there's nothing to be scared about alright? Because I'll be there with you and I won't let anything bad happen to you. And we're not going to the hospital again for a long time, ok?"

He sighed. "Ok."

"How are your eyes feeling by the way? They hurt at all?"

"No."

This is something we try not to ask him on a daily basis, but we do. Something about the pressure build-up. A bad sign.

"Hey," I say, trying to smile. "You know your dad will always protect you, right?"

"Like a shield or whatever?"

"Yeah, like Captain America's shield. Nothing gets through big dad."

He thought this was funny and sort of laughed.

I told him I loved him and that he should give me a kiss. Then I hugged him and I thought about his eyes. I felt his heartbeat.

PREENING

MY BOY OFTEN pretends he is a blue jay by sitting in trees acting like a blue jay and hoping the other blue jays will notice his flawless interpretation of being a blue jay. When he wants to fly, he jumps down to the ground and runs around with his arms out saying "CAW! CAW! CAW! CAW!"

UNDERCOVER

WHEN I WAS nine, I went camping with my father near Mt. Hood. One evening while getting fresh Cherry Cokes from a nearby mountain stream he saw a bald eagle preening atop a half-carbonized tree.

"Fuck bald eagles," my father said.

I laughed.

"Fuck bald eagles," he said, gathering up the Cokes and karate kicking a tree, feeling excited about using the word "fuck" in front of his son.

Later my father put on a gray sweater. We ate chili by a fire. We talked about baseball. My father smiled. He was growing a beard. One day he would be smiling in the Denver Airport of Death, but today he was smiling under normal non-death conditions; breathing without making fearful choking faces, with his bowl of chili, and his facial hair, that together signified peerless health and stability or something like stability. My father's stability made me proud. I wanted to be like him and Steve McQueen from "Bullit." I wanted to wear dark blue turtlenecks and give a hard ass look at some D.A. who was trying to screw me over and just walk away even though I could probably knock him out with one punch if I wanted. My life should be like that, my nine-year old self thought. Eat fresh fruit off of beautiful women. Write long, thoughtful letters to my mother. Drive sports cars in the dazzling sunlight of Monaco, laughing.

FLUID DYNAMICS

WHEN DID I first hear of Dr. Haas?

The woman I kissed outside the hospital on 99th and Madison told me.

Her son's brain was trying to kill him, too.

It was close to midnight two summers ago. She was probably in her late thirties like me except with gray, almost white hair with hints of auburn, and incredible green eyes like two gobs of Burmese jade. There was a sort of unhinged buoyancy about her. Like the impending doom had somehow brought her to life instead of slowly letting the air out. She shared her last cigarette with me and talked about Dr. Haas as if he were from a distant planet put here to alleviate the immense, deep sea pressures of cerebrospinal fluid in our Earthling children.

Except he was from Austria.

For some reason, I liked the idea of someone named Haas. Haas who was from Austria.

He seemed real. He seemed like someone who would shake your hand in a firm but friendly way, then calmly look over some CAT scans as he lit up his meerschaum pipe.

I imagined Dr. Haas fly fishing for trout in the northern Bohemian forest when he wasn't figuring out rare brain diseases. Maybe that's all he saw out there. Tangled webs of cold mountain streams. Bottle-green fistulas gurgling and swirling down-current, forming life-threatening eddies and unwieldy rapids, all of it rushing off to somewhere vital and heartbreaking.

Then I kissed the woman against the wall of the hospital. Or maybe she kissed me.

It happened very quickly.

Afterwards she went to her hospital room with her sick boy and I went to mine.

LOTUS PART ONE

I MET MY wife in a Thai restaurant in the Tenderloin. I had just finished my first year with the SFPD. We had four drinks each and decided to move to Uruguay. It made sense. If we were eating French bistro, or Cuban it might not have made sense. We might have moved to Cleveland or started a death cult. In Uruguay, we would eat steak and have five balconies. We would have time to talk and to have sex and not think about things like arterial venous malformations.

My wife is smarter than me and beautiful, but she is also very sad. Even before our son's brain was trying to kill him, she would often moan in her sleep like an old tanker off Cape Horn or do the laundry with saltwater piling up in her eyes.

But over time her sadness was honed into a sharp thing to lash out with. It was weaponized. She was the Daisy Cutter of sadness.

Tears now are often followed by "Go fuck yourself" or looks like switchblades.

But it wasn't always like that. Early on her melancholy was supple and her despair full of tenderness.

"Do you think life will get easier?" she asked me once a long time ago, before moving to the diseased and misty north.

"I don't know," I said. "Maybe."

One time she said she wanted our first child to look like me.

"First?" I said.

"Fuck you," she said in a playful way.

"What about you?" I asked.

"I hate my lips. And my hair."

"I like your lips and your hair."

She took a deep breath. Her eyes didn't roll, but they almost rolled.

LOTUS PART TWO

SEVENTEEN DAYS BEFORE I left with our son for Guatemala, my wife and I had cocktails at a friend's house, followed by an argument on the way home.

"That's my privacy," I yelled.

"Oh Christ," she said.

Always the rolling of eyes.

Always the snorting of nose.

MAROONED

MOST OF THE TIME she got her way. The school. The wallpaper. The turkey meatballs. But one day I came home to find new deck furniture arranged outside. It was big orange composite furniture that clashed with the light blue trim on our house. It's hard to explain, but somewhere in my bones a decision was made. I went out onto the deck, took one of the chairs and threw it into a hedge like I was tossing an unwanted fish back into the sea.

"Fuck that," I said to the chair in the hedge.

For a while I just stood there and looked at it sitting in the bushes, it's life upended. It gave me a deep satisfaction.

When she came home, she asked why there was a chair in the hedge, and I told her the furniture had to go.

"Jesus, just say you don't like it," she said.

"I will next time you ask me, darling," I said, striding out into the latest flash flood.

Another time my wife and I fought about syrup.

I wanted the authentic kind from Vermont, which was more expensive, and she wanted Log Cabin. I told her, "Log Cabin, really?" and she threw the Log Cabin at the soup aisle and left.

This was our second date.

I followed her outside. It was a wintry June morning in San Francisco, and I felt panicked like I was having some kind of minor heart failure that would end in the possible coldness of an ambulance, saying, "Yes, I understand. Yes, I want you to cut my clothes off with scissors." I could feel the gills of my heart press against my ribcage. I was disgusted at myself for wanting more expensive syrup from Vermont. As we walked through the freezing sunshine, I said I was sorry. Later we had sex and I took three Polaroids of her wearing a cowboy hat and gray panties that had black horizontal stripes on them. We ordered Chinese and watched a movie. We laughed about the syrup. We always laughed back then.

COCKTAIL HOUR

I LOOK OUT on the front lawn. I have a margarita. It is yellow and green and tastes like spring sunshine. I think about death as I wave hello to a family on their way to the shore. They've thought about death, I think, as I wave. They've been alone in a small bedroom, or a car stuck in traffic. They've looked at the grass, and seen the sunlight, and thought about how all of them go under the little white flowers and the grass and the ocean and they're dead like steel or like disco. But right now, is different. It's a picnic. Or a board game. Or yelling at their progeny deep inside some closet on Christmas Eve, then belting a martini after. Or two. You feel bad. You feel it all going and you know you're just another person doing the same thing. It's boring and frightening at the same time. They don't know. Do they? No. They don't know at all, and that's why you pretend. That's why you stuff an avocado in your mouth crying at the window looking out at the lumps in your yard. White garage. Blue trim. Then just gray till the airplanes and the stars and the world falling away to somewhere we'll never see and don't want to anyway.

Every morning I put on my uniform and try not to think about it. I can't always be thinking about it. I need to do other things in life besides always thinking about it. I need to buy a gas grill. I need to have people over for gas grilled salmon with maybe a little wild rice and some expensive butter from Belgium and talk about politics or whatever the fuck just happened in Florida.

What did I expect? Controlling life? Manipulating it in some way so that endovascular abnormalities become extinct like 13-foot butterflies?

Sometimes I put a little whisky in my coffee and drive around the island with the CB off. I know all the secret spots to drive like a total maniac. I feel reckless about life. I feel like a movie where my friend pulls me aside one night and says, "Hey, I think you're being kind of reckless about life. Maybe we should go home." But instead of listening, realizing your friend only wants to help, you drink a bottle of Cutty Sark and smoke a Dutchmaster backwards while dancing on top of a glass top coffee table.

But then you remember this isn't a movie. It's a dumb, speeding monolith bereft of logic, or empathy.

Alexander I got bit to death by a monkey.

Jim Bowie died in his underwear.

One time two girls with a little brochure that purported to know what God thought about life and death came to my door.

It was a Saturday morning when they came. I had a bloody Mary and was wearing socks and a robe when I answered the door. The police chief of an entire island. My wife and son were off visiting her mother. In the background was a football game taking place in the quiet blizzard of the Midwest. The girls were dressed up as if they were going to church or someone's funeral. They were young. Probably high school. They handed me the brochure. They looked at the lumps in our yard and then me in my socks with my morning cocktail, sort of trying to understand what made them different from me.

It was a rainy winter day.

Before they could say anything, I laughed and threw the brochure on the porch.

It was the right thing to do.

You can't explain the nature of oblivion.

Not to a man in a robe, drinking vodka before lunch.

FULL SPEED AHEAD

MY BUDDY MARTY who has the cocaine problem, but is my best friend from high school, and pretty good with his 68-foot longline trawler, has invited me for a drink next to his stool at The Goose Bottom.

"Oh, chief," he says, gripping two schooners of beer he's ordered for himself. "Tonight, we have an eighty percent chance of Aztec skulls floating over that pool table as they hum something catchy in Portuguese. And now to Rob with sports. Rob, can you hum in different languages?"

I hum.

Marty laughs because he is talking about sunshine acid.

He gets a kick out of it. Just talking about sunshine acid with his best friend, the chief of police. He read it in an article somewhere. Talking about how you can buy it easy on the dark web now, like everyone nowadays is some kind of disgraced CIA agent running an opium den a couple clicks outside Vientiane.

Without telling Marty, I will actually order acid online the next day.

This is something he will never know. My wife. My family. My department. No one will ever know this about me.

Beforehand, I will read one or two articles on the internet somewhere and log in or on the dark web and find acid I can buy with bitcoins. I will find the cheapest, smallest amount of acid and buy that. Then I will get a PO box at the post office on the mainland. Two weeks later a letter will arrive from *The Law Offices of Garabino, Shad, And Tuck*. It will have a stamp with a cartoon heart on it and the word "Love" over the heart like it is made of letters that have been individually inflated somehow. Inside will be a fake letter. Inside that will be a micro-Ziplock containing tiny strips of thin white cardboard, which I'll cut up into micro-doses, which are about five cuts per strip.

Then I'll try two of the strips.

It's pretty good acid, I'll think, because my heart will expand in waves of pink saltwater, softly choking out the sound of my siren as I climb to 97mph down Harrison at lunch hour.

I will live at this speed forever.

I will feel Guatemala somewhere deep inside my plasma.

I will feel my son's pulse like a never-ending detonation.

WHAT A DYING HOMELESS PERSON SAID TO ME ON MY FIRST DAY AS CHIEF

"WHEN YOU GO down hard you will know it because it is usually the last time you go down. To see what will happen and who will be happy and who will live without the house being emptied, the dog being put down, the dartboard in an old stereo box bound for Goodwill. The mother. The sink with the fucked-up tooth in it. There's no stopping them."

RETURN OF FISH MAN

MARTY WAS LIKE a fish growing up. He could swim like a fish. He smelled like a fish. He slept with fish. He even looked a little like a fish. But then he didn't want to be a fish anymore and moved away and got into car sales in Seattle. He sold used Mercedes. He didn't see the point of swimming anymore. Sometimes he held his breath in the shower just to see if he still had what it takes, but never the ocean. At night, he ate beef flavored Top Ramen and did blow off a coffee table book about different kinds of bridges. Eventually he sold a Mercedes to his future wife. They drove around in the Mercedes doing blow all the time and wearing leather and fucking like it was the 1980s. But then two weeks before they got married, he found out she had been seeing her old boyfriend for almost a year and Marty called off the wedding. The wedding was supposed to be on Maui. Then he decided since everyone had already bought their tickets and their rooms that everyone on his side of the aisle would still go to Maui for a three-day party instead. My wife and I were there from San Francisco. Everything was less complicated then. Beneath the palm trees and the water falls we consumed massive amounts of rum while dancing and bodysurfing.

Years later, Marty confided in me that he intended to commit suicide on the last night by jumping from his hotel balcony into the Pacific Ocean below, but for some reason, after looking down into the blue swirling surf he decided to move back to Wolf Island and work on the family fishing boat until he made enough to buy his own.

"The Pacific Ocean saved my life," he told me once with fish-like reverence.

3:07 AM

I WAKE UP in the middle of the night and walk down to the kitchen to find some Old Fitz, or a little sherry. I pour some and check on my son who is fast asleep. Outside there are clouds and the moss and the werewolves hunting my son's cerebellum. I bend down. I kiss the part where his little shoulder meets his neck.

I put on a big Pendleton blanket and go to our deck.

Moonlit roofs peek over the dark trees like shrinking blue glaciers. Our lumpy backyard goes out to a small thicket of rhododendron and sticker bushes where my son has a fort made of old trellis with little six-penny nails sticking out. Past that is the Hendricks place. A tall stand of oak. Then beyond the trees and Padilla Bay is Guatemala.

It's just a bit of water and then Guatemala is just there, waiting.

My son's life as a tax attorney or stunt driver lies somewhere out there. Somewhere in the jungle, just below the volcanoes and the jaguars and the tamarind trees.

I go back to sleep.

The next morning, I get up while my wife goes jogging and make a fried egg for my son. I eat nonfat yogurt with dehydrated organic cranberries. I try to smooth my son's hair with water from the sink then take him to school. Afterwards I check my phone for airfare to Guatemala and laugh out loud in my patrol jeep.

"Fucking Guatemala," I say to my Wonder Woman coffee mug.

Just then an SUV speeds past doing over 70 in a 35.

I turn on the siren.

When I walk up the man says his kid broke his leg falling down the stairs and he's taking him to the hospital. His son looks a little like my son. The way he tries not to cry.

"So, what's the damage?" the dad asks.

I tell him no ticket. And next time he wants to get to the hospital without getting pulled over to take Harrison.

"Thanks, chief," he says, driving off with his son who finally lets out a wail.

COLD FEET

HAVE YOU EVER seen a dead boy? They lie in the surf, or in their beds undisturbed. They have on little shirts and shoes, but maybe one shoe is missing. Maybe one eye is open. You want to pick them up and kiss them on the cheek. You want to play catch with them, but they just lie there. At one time, you saw them run up the stairs. They had wild hair and wild eyes. They would be pilots and construction workers, and three feet taller and not lying face down in the sand as the tide comes in. When you see a dead boy, you can't understand how he is dead. It doesn't seem right. It seems like he should be running and falling down and crying about something and growing older and fishing with you and watching a show on TV with you even though he has somewhere better to be instead of just under thirty-six inches tall and not breathing. When my son went into surgery, they let us see him one last time and all I could see were his feet sticking out from under the blanket. They wouldn't let the father in. Just the mother. She got to kiss him. All I could see were his feet that sort of lolled out sideways from the drugs. I remember thinking he was still alive then. I could tell them to stop and to turn the machines off and he would still be alive and talk to me and I could kiss him. But then he would probably die. Maybe he would die the next day. Or in two months. So I didn't say anything. I just went along with it because that was the best thing for him, even though it meant I might not be able to talk to him again or to look in his eyes and know it was my boy looking back at me and not some lifeless stare. He has big cheeks. He has the kind of eyes that smile. That's rare. I never want to lose that. I never want to see his body look small and unmoving. If I see that everything would change. I would stop looking people in the eye. I would be a person that other people wouldn't understand.

SEA CHANGE

I WAKE UP in the middle of the night again because of the phone. It's The Goose Bottom. Marty needs to be picked up.

The same Marty who once swam naked from Wolf Island to Priest Point after a twelve-pack of Rainier. The same Marty who drove his dad's truck onto the golf course to prove the "existence of turtlenecks."

I drive over and the great Marty slumps into the passenger seat.

"Are we still the same kind of friends we were in high school, or has something changed that is irreversible?" he says looking out the window as I drive along the coast, thinking the sea air will do something for him.

"I guess we've changed," I say. "We're older."

"Lots of shit has happened alright. But that shouldn't change the basic nature of our friendship, should it? Having a drug problem, trying to write poetry about goblin sharks, job status, that seems beside the point, no?"

"Except those things can add up and ultimately change people and people are what make friendships tenable or not tenable."

"Have I changed? I mean to the point that our friendship is no longer tenable?"

"I don't think so."

"I asked because sometimes people don't ask and they're surprised later to find out everything they thought was wrong. Because I know I can always count on you and you don't usually judge me, at least to my face, and hopefully you know you can count on me no matter what. With your work. Your boy. Whatever."

"Thanks."

"Can we pull over here?"

"Why?"

"I think I need to puke."

BITTER PILL

PEOPLE SAY YOU choose your friends, but most of the time it feels like they choose you. I didn't choose my son, but I like him. I mean I love him obviously, in a fatherly way, but that doesn't necessarily mean you like someone. I genuinely like my boy. He's sweet-natured and has a way of looking at things that make me smile.

He calls his lungs his "lums."

He doesn't eat spicy things because he says his "taste bug" doesn't like them.

I asked him once what he wanted to be when he grows up.

"I want to be a pilot," he said, "'cept I don't want to fly by myself."

"You want a co-pilot?" I said.

He nodded and pointed at me. For some reason, it reminded me of the hospital when he was too tired to speak. He would eat applesauce and watch cartoons. We would all watch cartoons together. On the worn blue couch with the heavy rayon heart. Then he would get bored and we would read him books. Books about trains and dogs and pirates that had trouble spelling. Nurses came and went. Down the hall you heard screams of other children. You heard nurse shoes hurrying somewhere to alternately make the screams go away or make them louder. When I'm 78-years old and dying of some sort of ultra-resistant anal cancer I will remember the sound of nurse shoes. The sound of cartoons and children wailing at four in the morning. I will remember the cheap hospital pajamas and the little disposable socks with the rubber soles so they don't slip on the shiny gray floors with their IVs and electrical machines trailing behind them in a procession of beeps and soft gushing noises.

Sometimes my son would throw his Hot Wheels across the room, crying from boredom or pain.

I would drink whisky out of a paper cup in the bathroom, quietly saying "fuck you" to the hospital.

The hospital was not a building but breathing and pulsing with life.

I wanted to wrap my arms around it in a sleeper hold and hug it tighter and tighter until it no longer pulsed, and one by one the lights would go out.

No one would come to the hospital's grave, or speak at its funeral, I thought.

No one liked hospitals.

COLLISION

LISTENING TO TAJ MAHAL and reading *The Seattle Times* with a quarter-dose of acid. Things just shimmering a little around the edges. Half dose?

My son is playing with his cars. A terrible pile-up near the fireplace where doubtfully anyone has survived.

My wife comes in with a steaming cup of tea. She is leaving me.

"It'll just be for a few days," she says, forgetting how we used to laugh in Chinatown after too much snake wine. "We're going to stay with my mom in Palm Springs next week. I think we need time to think on our own. Or I need time to think. I'm just so fucked by all this. We're not doing well, you know?"

I had heard about this. About how a high percentage of couples going through a traumatic illness with their child are more likely to go to Palm Springs and live with their mothers.

I once saw a woman stab her husband in the ear with a letter opener. Afterwards, when she was in cuffs she began crying and telling him she loved him as he bled all over their white shag carpet.

I tell my wife I understand. Or maybe I just nod.

After dinner, I ask if she wants to watch a movie. She is looking out the window, clenching and unclenching her jaw. I can see her laptop is open to a Facebook group devoted to parents of children with body parts that are trying to kill them.

"We have to think about what we're going to do," she says finally breaking her gaze.

"I know," I say.

She goes upstairs and sleeps next to our boy, which she does almost every night now.

I go outside and smoke a cigarette.

I smoke in the bushes where no one can see me.

THE GOVERNOR OF OAKLAND

A TYPICAL MORNING for the police chief of Wolf Island involves visiting people who smoke crack and live in apartments that smell like old tuna. I'm supposed to help these tuna-smelling people. Just the other day I went to an apartment on the far side of the island where two hookers lived to see if they'd visited the jobs office. One hooker was Inuit and the other was white and they had been charged repeatedly with being hookers. It was ten in the morning and in between answering questions the hookers would drink Almaden blush while watching the "Price Is Right" at abnormal volume levels. When someone won, the white hooker would look at me and say, "How fuckin' retarded, right?"

But that's nothing.

One time when I was still a cop in San Francisco a guy in the back of my cruiser thought the "governor of Oakland" was fucking his wife while he served time for trying to burn down a telephone booth. Another time a prisoner stole his cellmate's Jell-O so the next day his cellmate stabbed him repeatedly with a broom handle during movie time, except all the guards were busy setting up the VCR for "The Empire Strikes Back," so no one found him until much later on when he'd already lost a lot of blood and had to have his arm amputated from the elbow down because his arm had also been repeatedly stabbed.

Most of the time though I took pictures of bloody doorknobs. Or I talked to people named Mr. Ron. Mainly I talked to drug dealers, and child-abusers, and aggravated assaulters.

Then we moved to Wolf Island and got the house with the big Asian maples. I was done with those people. I craved small town drunk-and-disorderlies and folks complaining about their neighbor's tree branches.

My last day on the job before moving north I went to one of the tiny interview rooms at the county jail in San Bruno to talk to an attempted murderer. His name was Donald. He was a big Irishman who said hello and sat down like he wasn't a racist who attempted to run over a homeless black man with his truck two nights ago.

"Do you know who I am?" asked Donald.

"You're Donald," I said.

"I'm not really Donald."

"Who are you?"

"I'm a werewolf."

"___."

"Give me a piece of paper," said Donald.

"Why?" I said.

"My claws hurt."

I handed him some paper. Donald drew on the paper with his fingernail. He gave it back to me, but it was blank.

"What's this?" I said.

"Read it when there's a full moon," said Donald.

"Why?"

"I guess that's only the time you can read it or whatever."

"Ok."

"You don't believe me."

I shrugged.

"Look at my eyes," Donald said.

Donald opened his eyes wide, but they looked like regular eyes to me.

"Not all werewolves are bad, but some are," said Donald.

"Why are you telling me this?"

"Because of something you're going to do."

"What?"

Donald stood up.

"You shouldn't go to the jungle," said Donald.

"What jungle?" I said.

Donald walked to the door where the guard was waiting.

"If you go to the jungle they'll probably do something," said Donald.

"Who will?" I said.

"Good luck," said Donald.

YOMIKO

ONE MORNING WHILE dreaming of Guatemala, I see a red sedan pull out of a coffee drive thru. At a distance, I can see long grayish-white hair blowing in the wind.

I know right away it's her.

The woman from 99ᵗʰ and Madison.

She bolts through an intersection, but the light turns red. I don't have time to wait. I put on the siren, tires screeching. As I weave through traffic, I try to think of what I'll say to her. Why is she here? Has she seen Dr. Haas? Does she even remember me?

Then I lose her.

I hit the brakes.

I scan the street for the red car, but nothing.

Then I see an alleyway up to the right and stomp the gas, hoping for a break. I cut off another car and barrel through a trash can when I see the red car again. It's stopped now, having probably heard the siren.

I pull up behind and get out.

It feels like 99th and Madison all over again, but instead of Central Park it's trash bins surrounding the back entrance of a condemned seafood restaurant.

At first, I feel excited, but as I walk up to the red car, I can feel something is wrong.

Her grayish-white hair is not acting right. It looks different. The way it fell on her shoulders or maybe the tint of the grayness was off, darker somehow.

Finally, I get to the driver-side window and realize the problem.

The woman from the hospital is an old man.

"What did I do?" he says. "Did I not signal?"

"Your hair," I tell him.

"What about my hair?"

"Sorry. I thought you were someone else."

I tell him he can go.

Then my phone rings.

I answer, still shaking my head at chasing an old man at high speed down an alley, knocking over trash cans like some 80's cop show.

"Is this Chief Bell?" a woman's voice says.

"Speaking," I say.

"This is Dr. Yomiko."

"Doctor who?"

"Yomiko. I am assistant to Dr. Haas. I am meeting with possible candidates for treatment in Seattle this week. Sorry so last minute, but we have to do things this way. Can you be available?"

OREGON ROUTE 140

I TELL MY wife there's a police chief conference I forgot about and leave the next day. I tell her I'll be back before they leave for Palm Springs. I buy a train ticket at King St. Station and sit next to the window. I wonder if the woman from 99th and Madison will be there. I watch the early morning trees and the mist go by, the passenger car filling with smells of black coffee and wet newspaper.

Later in life I probably won't live on Wolf Island, I think.

I'll live in a cave behind Deep Creek Falls. I'll watch the water rip past in white bubbling sheets when I'm not watching PBS, or college football on my flat screen TV that I've expertly hammered into the basalt wall. I'll have a living room with a bookshelf and a nice bear rug to warm the place up. On holidays my son will visit with his family. They'll jump off the top of Gibson Canyon and I'll catch them through the water, and we'll eat trout amandine and roast cliff swallow with some

Middle Eastern spices. Later my son and I would sneak off to fish from a nice dry ledge somewhere and drink calvados. Talk about life. Who got promoted? Who died? Who cleaned out their wife's savings and skipped town to become an ice aficionado in Tierra del Fuego?

Marty wanted to go to Seattle with me as "backup," but I told him to stay and keep an eye on the island for me.

"Ok," he said, "but you don't know who the fuck this Yomiko character is. Classic shanghai situation if you ask me."

I told him I'd bring my Beretta, but I didn't.

I really don't like guns. I suppose the possibility of death petrifies me in a way unbecoming of a police chief. I don't look inside body bags like they do so casually on TV cop shows. I always send deputies to the morgue.

Once in San Francisco I was shot at, but I could tell he didn't really want to shoot me. He was just scared and probably on meth or something. He said he came from the Sea of Tranquility. I talked to him before the SWAT team came in to blast his brains back to the moon, and everything worked out.

Afterwards I told my wife over warmed up pizza and she cried and kissed the top of my head over and over and I told her everything was alright, but I didn't want her to stop.

It's sad if I let myself think about it. Looking at the way we are now. That moment in our apartment in San Francisco will never change, of course, icebound in time and space, but the people who lived that moment, those people have changed, which in a way changes the subtext of that moment, altering its meaning in some way so that it is less powerful now, quaint.

"Those two must be living an incredible love-filled life together," you would have exclaimed if you happened to be there, in that moment, except my wife and I are the moment's only living witnesses.

It will die with us.

I look out the train window at the present tense rushing by in vibrant blues and greens.

I drink my coffee.

I eat some nonfat yogurt.

LITTLE WAVES

MY WIFE AND I once walked down to the ocean. This was in another part of the world in another time. Before Guatemala. Before suicidal brains. We swam out until we were up to our necks. My wife straddled me. We did it as slowly as possible so her friends on the beach wouldn't see. Afterwards my wife and I went back to our respective chaise lounges. We fell asleep in the sun dreaming of things that would never happen.

APHOTIC

OF THE FIVE widely recognized oceans I had always heard the Atlantic was the most demanding ocean. The Pacific had all the looks and personality, but when push came to shove the Atlantic would shove you out the front door of your own home and beat you senseless in front of the neighbors.

It has a coldness to it, the Atlantic. Like some figure at the end of a dark alley slowly slapping a crowbar into his palm.

I sometimes think of the Atlantic when I think about my son.

The coldness of his disease.

The malformation hiding deep in the darkness of his brain like an iceberg waiting to sink us all. Does that make sense? If I can define it that will help him in some way. I can't shoot it in the face, or talk it down, so that will be my way of being useful. That's the thing, really. We all become so pathetic when we care. That's when hearts break. That's when hopes gently descend into the midnight zone, giant squid and angler fish, everything bathed in accelerating blackness.

That's where the sunlight ends.

CARTOGRAPHY

I HAD HEARD Dr. Haas lived on a remote volcano overlooking a lake in the Guatemalan Highlands of the Sierra Madre de Chiapas, and that he sometimes performed his surgeries in the open mountain air.

I also heard he had been chased out of Austria. Then somewhere in Africa for practicing medicine without a license.

Some call him a murderer. Others call him a saint.

The woman who I kissed on 99th and Madison drew me a map on the back of the New York Post, showing me where he was. As she drew it against the wall of the hospital, I watched her cigarette dangle from her mouth in a surprisingly elegant way. She even made the tired yoga pants she was wearing seem elegant. When she was done drawing, we heard thunder not far off. It was about to rain. A summer storm from the vast, gimlet-eyed Atlantic.

"The roads are pretty bad, but I think there's a train," she said, handing me the map. I noticed she had good penmanship, which in some way comforted me about the future in general. I imagined my four-year old son and I on the back of some rickety bus, climbing through the cloud forest. Green, green, blue, dark green. Not long after that the woman kissed me.

Or I kissed her.

For some reason, I think about all this as I take the elevator to the 23rd floor of the Mayflower Park Hotel.

Dr. Yomiko is waiting there.

YOMIKO NUMBER 2

I AM IN a suite overlooking the Space Needle, talking with a Japanese woman, who is wearing an earpiece and a tight red and blue dress that makes her look like a tin of expensive Italian tuna.

"Your boy is how old again?" asks the woman.

"Four," I say. "Four-and-three-quarters, actually."

"How many surgeries?"

"Six."

"All for the Vein of Galen Dalmation?"

"Malformation? Yes."

"Sorry, I didn't—sorry."

"It's alright. What's your name again?"

"Oh, it's—sorry, you can call me, Dr. Yomiko."

"Cut the shit," I tell her. "You're no doctor."

I get up to look around the place.

"Excuse me," the woman says. "Who do you think you're talking to?"

"Most likely a hooker with a hearing aid."

The hooker looks very serious all of a sudden. They must've paid her a lot of money to be so serious, I think. Dr. Yomiko is probably somewhere else, listening, watching.

"Where's the doctor?" I say. "Where's the real Yomiko? Where is Dr. Haas?"

The hooker pauses as she listens to her earpiece.

"You're the policeman, aren't you?" she says.

"I'm the chief of police of an island up north," I say. "Who gives a fuck? I'm here for my son."

"Do you want a drink?"

"Sure," I say feeling angry and a little out of control. "Why the fuck not?"

The hooker goes to the bar. "Whisky?"

I nod, looking around the room, which is spotless.

The hooker pours something from a crystal decanter. "What did Dr. Harrison in New York say about your son's last surgery?"

"How did you know about Harrison?"

"What did he say?"

She hands me the drink and I watch her as I swallow it.

"That he almost died," I say feeling the anger slide out of me. "They punctured something in his brain. He went blind for a while. They're still watching him for hydrocephalous."

"Did they say what percentage of the malformation is left?"

"Less than ten percent, but I guess it's pretty deep, near the cortex. I don't know. Listen, when am I going to meet Dr. Haas?"

"Don't worry. Dr. Yomiko is here. She can hear you. Did you bring the latest scans?"

I hand the hooker a manila envelope with the scans.

She hands me a post card of Archduke Ferdinand. On the back it reads:

*April...$25,000...**Antigua, Guatemala...Casa** Encantada...**Patience is a virtue.***

THE LUMINAIRES

THE WOMAN FROM 99th and Madison is in the lobby when the elevator door opens. Her gobs of green jade are watching me as I walk up to her not sure what to say.

"Did you meet her?" she says, looking very pretty. Like Bora Bora, I imagine she will be very pretty for a very long time. She has a touch of sadness, too, but there's no anger behind it. It's a pure and good-natured melancholy that likely embraces all maple syrups of the world.

"Hi," I say.

"Oh, hi," she says, blushing.

"Yes, I met her. You?"

"Yeah. Are you…with your family?"

"No, you?"

"No. They're back in Denver."

"I just came down a few hours north of here."

"It must be a regional thing," she says wondering aloud. "It makes sense they wouldn't go town to town for each family."

"You have a son, right?"

"Yes."

"Same."

"I remember. My name is Katherine. I don't think we ever properly, you know."

"Tom. Tom Bell."

"You want to get a drink, Tom?"

We drink at the hotel bar in a high booth.

Back home my wife is packing for Palm Springs. Sticker bushes and sogginess pressed against the storm windows.

There are three other people drinking at the bar.

Maybe one of them has a child like ours, I think. Slowly dying somewhere faraway like Bismarck or Lake Charles. Or maybe their sons are normal and they're just having normal drinks. Sometimes I can remember what normal feels like, but usually it feels just out of reach, like an old photograph of you at some dinner party you don't recall, but you're there in the photograph eating some sort of quiche so you must've been there.

Katherine and I talk about Dr. Haas and our sons and keep ordering drinks until it is late in the evening. In between drinks I catch her drawing a map of Guatemala on her cocktail napkin.

She's a believer like me.

Believing in things is rare and powerful like uranium.

I think about telling her I'm a chief of police, but why? She tells me she has a room for the night, so we order dinner up to her room. I call my wife from the hall and say, "I won't be home tonight after all. Just having drinks with some colleagues then I'll crash at the hotel."

The two of us go up to her room.

We eat dinner and then we turn off the lights and get into bed. We drink Old Fashioneds and look out the big windows at the nighttime city of Seattle, twinkling like a luxury cruise ship slowly passing.

"When are you going?" says Katherine.

"April."

"Us too."

"Maybe I'll see you there."

"Maybe our sons will become friends."

Katherine lies her head on my shoulder.

"Do you ever feel like what you do isn't really you, but you keep doing it anyway?" she says.

I wanted to pull the covers over us so our bed would turn into a submarine that we could ride into Guatemala together. Our sons would become fast friends. At night, we would turn on the floodlights and watch the krill and the goblin sharks, and I would hold her just like this, and take one more sip of my drink before leaning over her in the darkness.

MONOGAMY

I WALK DOWN the next morning from the Mayflower Park Hotel, following the hooker who is pretending to be a brilliant neurologist. She has on a different tight dress, electric blue, that makes her look like a surgeonfish, which are primarily found in the Indian and Western Pacific Oceans. They are sometimes hookers pretending to be brilliant neurologists, but typically they are herbivores who prefer monogamy to forty-dollar hand jobs.

In the early sun falling between clouds I am her predator.

I am her barracuda.

I follow her under the highway to the waterfront before she enters another hotel. I follow her inside. She walks up to a distinguished Japanese woman in a dark gray suit and they exchange envelopes.

"Hi everybody," I say to Dr. Yomiko, walking up behind them.

Dr. Yomiko turns as the hooker darts away into a dark lagoon of elevators.

"Chief Bell, how nice to meet you."

"I just wanted to see for myself, that you're real."

"I'm real," says Dr. Yomiko.

"And what about Dr. Haas? Is he real?"

"He is indeed real, chief. Will we see you and your family next month?"

"Maybe," I say. "I think so, yes."

EVENINGTIDE

THE SHIP IS named after an imaginary woman. Anna Marie is Marty's first wife, and the Anna Marie II is his second chance at not fucking everything up.

The ship is white and looks like an upside-down church. The deck is like a sacrificial altar to the Western Pacific. We're drinking sanctimonious light beer with the old ropes and sun-blasted piles of fish guts. I haven't worn my badge in almost three days now.

I open another light beer.

I am waiting for Guatemala to happen.

My wife and son are away, currently surrounded by juice fasting retreats, self-hating yogis, and an insatiable death-heat. My mother-in-law is in Palm Springs, too. She always liked me deep down, but there was only one move for her to make. She is making a second margarita for my wife about now. They are talking about how I have a tendency to be anti-social, or that I'm trying to kill our son, as the bone-white desert pulses and melts all around them.

"Did you see the skeleton of that horse?" says Marty, who is on acid again. "It looked like it was trying to get up, but something was wrong with it and it didn't get up. Like it hadn't planned properly, you know?"

"I think my son is going to die," I say.

Marty throws his beer at a seagull, or maybe a star.

"Fuck that," he says.

"Will you help me?"

"Help you what?"

"How long does it take this thing to go about two-thousand miles?"

Marty looks down at the old rope and the fish guts, then takes a deep breath like he just saw someone bet their mortgage on black.

WHITE TAIL

I WAKE UP behind the wheel of my patrol jeep with blood in my eyes. Sargent Patterson is there with his flashlight shining in my face.

"What the fuck?" I say to him.

"Chief, you ok? I think you ran off the road."

"It was a deer."

"A deer?"

"Yeah, a fucking deer."

I like Patterson. We have beers every-once-in-a-while and his wife used to be friends with my wife before she stopped being friends with people. I smile at Patterson.

"It's ok Patterson," I say. "I just need a little bandage is all. Just a cut."

While Patterson patches me up I lean up against his cruiser and light a cigarette.

"Where were you?" asks Patterson.

"Coming back from Seattle," I say. "Another doctor."

"How is your son?"

"He's good. He's fine."

Patterson finishes up and lights a cigarette, too.

"Maybe you should take a couple days, Tom," he says.

"Yeah, maybe I will," I say, watching the smoke float up into the sky like *SS Mont-Blanc*.

METEOROLOGICAL RECKONING

SPRING ON WOLF ISLAND is mostly lashing rain with intermittent salvos of sunshine. When my wife isn't in Palm Springs discussing the demise of our marriage over margaritas, we walk out into the woods with our son. He throws rocks against big Douglas Firs and out across the water. Like throwing TNT into a graveyard, the forest suddenly comes alive with terrible sound.

Mostly we watch the clouds.

We become meteorologists as we predict how long we have till the next downpour. Then we stop becoming meteorologists and become a married couple again. We talk about what we might cook for dinner. Or if we have any wine. Otherwise we don't talk. Not much, anyway. What is there to talk about? Afghanistan? The Javan rhino? We watch our son watch the squirrels. We watch him laugh and run up and down the trail. We sometimes hold hands out of habit, or to show him how nothing has changed. How we walk in the woods and everything is the same no matter how many times we walk in the woods.

Once, I even thought about living in the woods.

Just go inside a tree with my son where the Vein of Galen Malformation couldn't find him. Like a neurological Passover. We would grow old together and eat sap and berries and squirrel meat, then watch the days and evenings pass through a hole in the bark. A Sitka Spruce perhaps, or Tasmanian Blue Gum. We would live the way a Sitka Spruce lives. Breathe through our needles. Eventually we'd become almost part of the tree, like two oversized mushrooms that loved each other unconditionally.

Now in the woods by myself I think about them.

I miss them.

A drizzle starts so I go home and pour myself some Fitz.

THE DESERT IN WARTIME

I GET A call from Palm Springs.

"How are you?" she says.

"I'm fine," I say. "You?"

"We're swimming a lot in the pool. He likes walking down to the putting green and chasing the lizards. Lots of ice cream. You know, never ending."

"Yeah, but how are *you*?"

"We're going to stay a couple extra days here," she says ignoring my question.

"What about school?"

"I called them. It's fine."

"What about me?"

"I'm still trying to figure things out, Tom."

"Me too. Can't we do it in the same zip code?"

"I have a lot I want to talk to you about."

"Sounds like fun. Can I say hi to him? Have his eyes been hurting?"

"He's napping right now. I—I spoke with his doctors in New York and that's part of what I want to talk about."

"What did they say?"

"Let's talk when I'm back."

"They still don't want to operate, do they? What percentage did they give you this time? Did they say it's miraculously all of a sudden gonna close up shop and go home as long as they don't touch a fucking hair on his head?"

"I can't talk about it now."

"Your mom there?"

"Yes."

"You two crack into the chardonnay yet?"

"Fuck you."

"Darling, this isn't going to go away just because we want it to."

"Oh Christ."

"Listen, I don't want to get into all the experimental—."

"Tom, do not fucking bring up that Haas character. And I think we both know what's at stake here."

"Do we?"

"What do you think I've been doing the last couple of years? Relaxing? Making the easy decisions?"

"Well, honey, last I checked Palm Springs has a few more golf courses than cutting-edge pediatric neurological centers."

"Bye, Tom."

HOW TO GET PUT ON
ADMINISTRATIVE LEAVE

HOW I GET put on administrative leave begins in the jungles of Guatemala. My mind goes there. My mind just floats there in the humidity amongst the jaguars and limestone as I pour a highball of Fitz with just a splash of water to coax out its unrealized potential like an equatorial cave full of copper and cobalt.

After that I call Marty and tell him to meet me at The Goose Bottom, as I pour my second (fourth?) Fitz.

The Goose Bottom at midnight is mostly comprised of truck drivers and fishermen and people who've suddenly realized they never want to go home again.

Maria, the barkeep, says they have a deal on Olympia tall boys with a Jack back. I say, "You gotta deal there, Maria."

"On me, chief," she says.

Marty comes out of the bathroom breathing through his eyelids like a lava lizard. He's wearing a T-shirt with big block lettering on it that says, "Fuck the Luftwaffe."

"I think you should take it down a notch after this one," says Marty, as he wipes his nose of cocaine residue.

"Aye, aye," I say.

"The future will be full of lasers and disappointment," continues Marty. "Robotic cows and depressed Kevin James impersonators. Everyone reciting Jerry Maguire as they drive speedboats into the Academy Awards, laughing. Don't you agree, chief?"

"Agree with what?"

"That the saddest is yet to come?"

I nod, looking at myself in the mirror behind the bar to see if I'm sitting upright. I am suddenly struck by the idea of my son dying as if hearing about it for the first time. This happens quite often actually, and it's a realization best chased with high proof liquor. I drink down the Jack, still looking into the mirror as if I were looking at someone else, but who?

If there was a Wikipedia entry on "Island police chiefs who are beyond drunk:"

> The island police chief who is
> beyond drunk is a fairly common
> species, but rarely found outside
> their habitat: police cruisers or

*clapboard houses on Double Bluff
Hill overlooking Padilla Bay. Some
have been known to carry pistols
or blackjacks, but most can barely
find their wallet. When
approaching said species one
should never make sudden
movements, or especially bring up
their sick child in any form of
conversation, casual or otherwise.
Overall, the island police chief
who is beyond drunk is supremely
unpredictable.*

That's when an off-duty Sargent Patterson comes over with someone to say hi before leaving.

"Heya, chief," says Patterson. "Take it easy tonight. Oh, and this is Bill. Friend of mine. He's a cop over in Priest Point."

"Hey," says Bill. "Hope your kid's doing ok."

"What?" I say. "My what?"

"Your kid. You know, I hope he's doing better."

At this point the island police chief who is beyond drunk strikes without warning, leaving Bill from Priest Point on the ground with a busted-up nose, bleeding all over the floor.

"Go fuck yourself," says the unpredictable island police chief.

FAREWELL, GRASS

I READ THE sports page with some coffee, flexing the bruised knuckles on my right hand in between sips. Then I change the bandage on my forehead and start packing.

I get winter and summer clothes for my son and stuff them into a big army duffel with my own clothes including rain jackets, and thermal underwear. Sunglasses. Swimsuits.

I go to the store and get non-perishable items like soups and beans and boxes of spaghetti. I stock up on distilled water and Old Fitz.

I go to the bank and withdraw $25,000 from our savings.

I go to the attic for sleeping bags and lanterns and backpacks and a first aid kit and a box of 9mm ammo.

Everything is piled up at the bottom of the stairs like a half-assed supply depot. I look it for a while. Then I look at the empty house. Then the doorbell rings. I answer it. It's a girl scout with boxes of cookies. I sign up for half a dozen.

"Where are you going," she says, looking at the fire sale behind me.

"Oh, I can't tell you that," I say. "Then it wouldn't be a surprise."

Off I go to Marty's to store everything in the bottom of the Anna Marie II. He's having a morning beer, covered in blue paint, as he watches me from his "lawn couch," which is just a couch without goals or any real direction in life. That's why they get along so well, I think.

"Light winds out of the northeast the next few days," he says, looking out to sea. "Waves less than a foot or so."

I go home and clean up the house. Make it presentable. Make it look like it's the same person living there as when they left. Then I pour a Fitz and sit out on the wet grass between our big Asian maples, taking it all in. Goodbye, shrubbery! Goodbye, sticker bushes!

THE GRAND NORTH PACIFIC HOTEL

WHEN I WAKE up early the next morning we are a family again. It is the color of sea urchins outside as my wife makes eggs and toast. My son is smiling with freckles sprouted up across his cheeks and nose fresh from the desert sun. With him is a new Hot Wheels he got at the airport. A van with a surfboard in back that is currently parked beside his orange juice. The three of us eat breakfast together for what might be the last time.

"Is everything ok?" she asks.

"I think so," I tell her. "I missed you."

"Yeah, right."

I squeeze her by the shoulder, realizing I haven't touched her in weeks. "I really did," I say.

After we eat, I tell her I want to take him to school so we say goodbye and get in the car and drive away. I look at the house in the rearview mirror. I look at the lumpy yard and the trees until the ground rises up behind us and everything disappears like Pompeii. We hit the main road at the bottom of the hill and drive towards town.

Out across the marshland, Padilla Bay sparkles and shines like a foreign country protecting the life and liberty of its fish citizenry.

"Are your eyes bugging you at all today?" I ask as casually as possible.

"No," he says, then switching the subject. "I forgot I had school today." He looks up at me with the sweet face that almost died so many times in my lap while watching Wheel of Fortune above his bed in the Pediatric Intensive Care Unit.

"Yeah," I say. "But maybe we'll take a little field trip instead. Would you like that?"

His face is alive. His eyes look at my eyes.

"Where are we going?" he asks.

"The ocean," I say.

"What about mom?"

"She'll probably meet us later," I say looking straight ahead so the lie seems more casual, easier to accept somehow.

"But we didn't get to kiss her goodbye."

"Sorry, champ. We won't be gone that long."

"How come you don't kiss anymore?"

"Your mom?"

"Yeah. You used to kiss, but now you don't really."

I try to think of a way to turn this into an innocent joke, or explain how people can go from sex on a ferry in the Sea of Crete to acting like strangers at a bus stop, but I can't. He's too young for the nuance of tragedy. Besides this sort of tragedy moves slow like a glacier, and when you realize what's happened it's too late. I force a chuckle instead and turn on the radio. To show him how silly he's being. To show him all is right with the world and heartbreak is rare like moon rocks. I know at this point, sitting next to my dying son as we drive away from the love of my life, I should feel something. Something heavy giving way somewhere deep inside, behind the spleen, perhaps, or the superior mesenteric. But really that part of me gave way long ago. In a hospital elevator perhaps, or maybe that day at the beach, watching the water churn blue-green. Imperceptible fissures that were only visible by electron microscope.

And then came the Vein of Galen.

And then Dr. Haas.

And then the mowing of lawns.

She won't miss me, not this version anyway. But she'll miss him.

That's why I have to save him.

We meet Marty at the docks and climb aboard his upside-down white church, except it's now blue with white trim and looks like an upside-down post office. He's changed the name from Anna Marie II to Tiffany I.

"Who the fuck's Tiffany?" I ask the postmaster general of the sea.

"My first love, the slut."

As we slip out of the harbor, I think about getting my gun just in case someone follows us, but who would I shoot at? My wife? One of my deputies?

I feel the breeze on my face.

I smell the kelp and the mermaids washing their hair down below.

"There's no turning back now," says Marty, followed by a quick snort.

"Take it easy," I say.

"Of course, chief. You know me. Fit as a violin. I was thinking this sorta reminds me of a movie I once saw. Or maybe it's just like a movie. Like just the beginning of one you're not exactly sure of, but things look pretty good so far which means maybe at least the director knows what the hell he's doing."

"Are we having a sleepover on the ocean?" asks my son.

"You bet, kiddo," says Marty, cracking open a beer.

"How far do you think we'll get today?" I ask him.

Marty thinks about it as he takes a swig. "Probably close to Astoria, I guess."

I nod happily at this estimate. The Tiffany I is like our passport into this strange rippling country, as we plow further beyond the silvery borders of Wolf Island. I look around as if a tourist. We will visit the museums and historic landmarks of the Pacific Ocean. My son watches the water boil white beneath us. The gulls swoop down for fish, and he laughs.

"This is some of the nicest water you'll see," says Marty. "It reminds me of my ex-fiancé's inner thigh."

By lunchtime we push through the Strait of Juan de Fuca where we check into our rooms of the North Pacific. We have courtyard facing views of Cape Flattery. The king-sized waterbed stretches out for miles in every direction. From room-service I order up a peanut butter and honey sandwich for my son, and a corned beef for myself. We eat together, watching the birds swoop and the water churn. Deep down I'm afraid my son is dying. When he stops breathing, he will not look at me as I hold his face up against mine. His cheek against my cheek. He will just lie there. He will be gone. I will cry in someone's kitchen or hallway. I will cry in an Uber.

I look out at the Pacific Ocean.

I look at all the fish.

I look back at the way we came.

They must be in full alert mode now, I think. Roadblocks. APBs. Panicked phone calls to the neighbors.

"Feast your eyes on that Tiffany I!" Marty shouts. "That's open ocean my love, stretch your lovely legs!

PART TWO

NORTHEAST CORRIDOR

SHIPS ARE DRAMATIC things. The way the water and the men look against those big fireplace paintings of the sky.

Trains are dramatic, too.

The imagination required to tuck tunnels into breakneck cliff sides. The poetry of hundred-foot trestle bridges in a late summer squall.

After my son was first diagnosed, we ended up on a train to New York because our plane was forced to land due to weather. Some people had tickets to Aberdeen or Old Saybrook, but we took a train to our son's first brain surgery.

My son grabbed at his eyes and his head and tried to sleep in my wife's lap. Sometimes my wife and I looked at each other, but mostly we looked out the window imagining what this new life would look like. How would we act? What would we say when people asked us about it? Would we live in the same place? Wear the same clothes?

Would I still like tuna fish? Would we still say goodnight to each other in the same way? Would my son still play third base for Kansas City? Every once in a while, I would go to the bar car and order a double whisky, gulp it down, cry in the restroom for fifteen seconds then return to our seat and kiss him on the forehead where his brain was secretly trying to kill him. Then I would stare blankly out the window, or I looked at the other people on the train reading their books and staring at their iPads and thought it's not right that a one-year old should be dying here.

Why should a one-year old be dying next to a man doing spreadsheets on the outskirts of New Rochelle?

This was the wrong kind of train drama, I thought.

Train drama was gunplay on the Orient Express, or cheating on your wife somewhere between Wichita and Fort Worth on the Heartland Flyer.

Train drama didn't seem like it should be someone's father half-drunk in the bathroom that smelled of a thousand shits, crying silently into some brown paper towels as the night outside blurred by leaving in its wake a hundred old New Rochelles.

When my son finally fell asleep, I called the neurological team to let them know we would be at the hospital within the hour. They said admittance through ER would probably take an hour, another hour for prep then three hours or so for surgery.

It was six o'clock.

By midnight we'd know if my son would play third base or not.

All of Kansas City would fall asleep without ever knowing.

PEACEFUL SEA

THIS IS THE naval academy of rare brain malformations and Marty is Ferdinand Magellan raised from the dead for one last circumnavigation of pathophysiological death-defiance. San Francisco, Los Angeles, Todos Santos, Isla Maria Magdalena and Huatulco. Every shore will radiate like X-rays in the bony green distance.

Can you feel it? Can you hear the amniotic pulse?

Off the coast of California now. My son's face pointing towards Guatemala like a rare and beautiful compass. He's healthier on the move, I think. We all are. Velocity. Evolution. It's good for the blood.

"Are we going pretty fast?" asks my son.

"We are," I tell him.

"Do you think we're going faster than a motorcycle?"

"Oh yeah."

One time, far above 99th and Madison one of my son's doctors took me aside in a waiting area near a candy vending machine. It did not smell of sea air. There were no birds or tiny puffs of cloud overhead. Just a woman slumped in a chair softly crying behind us. The smell of warmed-over hospital food eddying under a gale of code blues.

"This morning your son underwent a combined transarterial and transvenous embolization of his VAGM," said the doctor. "The catheter access was achieved by passing the microcatheter from the arterial side into the recipient draining vein. We used Onyx, a liquid embolic agent to occlude fistulas comprising the malformation. We estimate about eighty percent occlusion has been achieved. Do you have any questions?"

"Yeah, when will he and I be able to go scuba diving off the Grand Banks?" I asked him. "When will he do this crazy spin move that no one sees coming and sack the rival team's quarterback thereby cementing his chances with the homecoming queen? When will he be able to take off that crappy hospital gown and put on his Captain America PJs and eat frozen waffles and watch whatever the fuck movie he wants in our bed back home? When will I stop trying to become a Navy Seal and driving a speedboat over an iceberg with the Dave Matthews Band? When will I stop eating avocados over the sink and sort of smooshing them into my mouth while crying uncontrollably?"

But I didn't ask any of those questions.

I just looked at the doctor and shook my head.

SAY HELLO

MY SON IS alive and we are now 2,292 nautical miles away from 99th and Madison heading south-southwest. Light variable wind. Sixty-two degrees.

I tell my son to say hello to the Pacific.

"Helllloooooooo!" he yells into the wind.

THE AUSTRIAN

THE STORM IS not the biggest storm Marty has ever seen. In fact, according to him it is only the seventh biggest storm next to the Bering Sea in '87, Bass Strait in '99, Gulf of Alaska in '01, Bering Sea in '02, Sea of Japan in '05, South Shetland Islands in '07, and Columbia River Bar in '12.

"The North Atlantic is a pussy!" he yells over the rain as he steers toward a rocky island for shelter.

"Where the fuck are we?" I yell back.

"Farallon Islands! Shark country!"

Marty looks like Christopher Columbus, but with dilated pupils and an increased risk of stroke.

I take my son below deck. We hide next to the little black oven with a ripped-out calendar page of Christy Turlington in galactic bondage hanging above it. My son watches me with a mix of terror and elation. He doesn't scare easily. One time at Disneyland the submarine broke down mid-ride and we had to wait for maintenance to get us out. Around the twenty-minute mark a couple kids began to lose it. One pounded against the hull screaming bloody murder. Another buried her head in her mother's lap saying "no" over and over again. But my son just sat there, patiently watching the same giant clam open and close, burping up big diamond bubble clouds towards the surface of Tomorrowland.

I smile at him, and he musters a quarter-smile back.

"D-dad?" he asks, starting to shiver.

"Don't worry," I tell him. "Just hang on to me, ok?"

Outside it sounds like a thousand car crashes going through the Monterey Bay Aquarium.

My son buries his head into my chest. I hold onto him, wondering how long we could survive in water like this. Maybe five minutes. Maybe less. Then I wonder how much further to Guatemala. He could die before he ever reaches the operating table. Then after a while it's suddenly a little calmer and I poke my head up to see if we're dead but find we're in a cove of some kind. There's even a dock there with another boat, the rocks on the cliffs all around us flickering under the fire-bolt sky.

Up on a hill someone is waving a flashlight at us.

117

We go towards the flashlight.

When we get there, we see a large woman in front of a small cabin, no bigger than a woodshed. She looks like someone's Midwestern mother had just been beamed there only seconds ago by aliens.

"Well, well look at you three," says the Midwestern mother recently beamed there by aliens.

Once inside we introduce ourselves and find out the Midwestern mother is actually a shark researcher named Nancy and that she has some leftover chili.

"I wish I had something for you to drink, but I ran out of whisky last week," she says making a pouty face.

"Ta-da!" says Marty, producing a pint of bourbon from his soaking jacket.

"Well, aren't I the lucky one," says Nancy.

We all drink bourbon and eat chili in the tiny, warm cabin.

My son crawls under some blankets and falls asleep in the bunk.

"So how many of you are out here?" I ask.

"Oh my, so many. And from all over, you know. My team is mostly from San Diego, but there's a South African team just down the hill from us, some Japanese scientists somewhere around here, and I even met a doctor from Austria the other day. I have no idea what he's studying."

"Sorry, you said Austrian?"

"That's him."

"Do you know what kind of doctor he is?"

"Gosh. Nope."

"Where is he?"

"He's on the other side of the island."

"Do you think we could see him tomorrow?"

"Well, I think he leaves first thing. At least that's what he told me."

"Which way is the other side of the island?"

"What do you mean?"

"I think he just wants you to point," says Marty, sighing a little, knowing he can't stop me.

"But you can't get there," says Nancy.

"Why?"

"You have to cross just a tiny little ridge and it's dark."

I take Nancy's flashlight and head out into the storm.

At first, I make good time, but then it gets steeper than an elevator shaft fairly quick. I'm basically tight-roping across a craggy rain-slick ridge that I can barely see. Japanese scientists at the bottom on one side and Great Whites on the other. I sort of do a shuffling sidestep while trying to keep a low center of balance. I do this for about two hundred yards when it begins to narrow, the edges crumbling on either side. And now the rain has lost its mind. Gusting at all angles. I keep looking down, wondering what it feels like to fall a hundred fifty feet then get chunked in half by two-ton sharks while drowning in fifty-degree water. But when I don't slip and get eaten while drowning I somehow end up at the front door of another cabin almost identical to the one before.

That's when it hits me.

All of a sudden in the middle of the seventh biggest storm in the history of coked-out fishermen, I'm not exactly sure what I am doing. Why would one Austrian doctor know another? It's a large country. With goddamn mountains. Also, why would I risk my life to find out?

I knock on the door anyway.

The mysterious Austrian who answers the door says his name is Dr. Bauer.

We sit by his stove.

"Yes, I know, Haas," says the mysterious Dr. Bauer who somehow knows the even more mysterious Dr. Haas. "Austria's not that big."

He gets up and goes to a bookshelf. He pulls something out of an old notebook and brings it back.

It's a black and white photograph. He points to two young men in a group of smiling young people, wearing thick sweaters at the foot of a mountain in the time of black and white photographs.

"That's us in 1966," he says. "We went to different schools obviously, but we knew some of the same people. We both liked to climb."

That's when I notice a naked Japanese woman in Dr. Bauer's top bunk. She's very pretty and at least half his age with nipples like flower hat jellyfish, jutting out pinkly into the soft lamplight.

"Oh, this is Dr. Oguchi," says Dr. Bauer. "She's very tired, aren't you doctor?"

"Yes doctor," says Dr. Oguchi, smiling, then putting on a T-shirt and quickly disappearing back under the covers like a buoy you see in a storm before being swallowed into another swell.

Dr. Bauer sits back down and produces a long pipe from underneath his chair, which he begins smoking.

"So, you know what Haas is capable of?" he says.

"No, what?" I say.

"His first operation took a man back to the summer of his eleventh year, the sunlight through a stand of Bald Cypress, the hot leather of his mother's Volvo station wagon."

He relights his pipe before continuing. "And no doubt you heard he once saved a young woman with an emotional transplant to restart her positive outlook on life. Not to mention the hundreds of children he's kissed on the forehead to turn them into future ornithologists and computer programmers with the healthy sex lives of Three Dog Night circa 1970."

A tiny giggle surfaces from the top bunk.

"Wait," I say. "Why are you fucking with me?"

"Because what you seek is bullshit," he says. "What you seek is a fantasy!"

I take the Austrian's pipe out of his mouth.

"Fucking doctors," I say, as I toss it in the fire.

Then I leave him and his nude Japanese scientist and walk out of there towards the craggy ridge of death.

Storms aren't so bad, I think to myself as I walk into the great dark morning rain of the Pacific Ocean, which is full of sharks and coked out fishermen and the future of pediatric strokes.

JELLYFISH BLUES NO.7

WE SAIL PAST the ICUs and rare diseases of San Francisco towards warmer zip codes brimming with sailfish and Bentfin devil rays. Every once in a while, we see small aircraft flying low and wonder if they're spotter planes. Marty says he even picked up some chatter about the Anna Marie II, but it was late at night and his clarity at those hours is up for debate.

"They can't be sure we're sailing all the way to Guatemala," says Marty, sensing my apprehension. "We could be going to Canada, then flying from there. We could be sailing to a remote island in the Aleutians to lay low for a few months with a couple runaway Inuit nymphos. Hell, you two could be on the road doing seventy-five just outside Billings and I'm out here all on my lonesome, decoying everyone, while secretly recording my seminal maritime-hillbilly album entitled *Jellyfish Blues No.7*. Think about it. Marty's on another bender, they'll say. Marty has no hopes or dreams. No strong opinions about the status quo. They'll shoot me on sight. Hang me from a shark cage and read something from Ashbery's *Self-Portrait in a Convex Mirror*. Goddamn, the torture will be exquisite!"

"Well, that and there's lots of ground to cover," I say, looking out at the vast ocean, stretching acetylene-blue in front of us.

Hundreds of miles already and hundreds more to go, I think. But no matter how far we go the ocean refuses to change. The same white-capped wavelets. The same fish. The same slippery sheen that looks intimidating at first, but after a while almost inviting, like a boundless meadow of gentle aquatic blue-grass where you could step right off the prow and lay into one of the cool rippling hills for a quick afternoon nap.

We don't see many people out here, which is good. Every time a plane or a boat appears on the horizon I make sure I'm within striking distance of my Beretta, and that my son is below deck. The closest anyone got was when one old trawler passed within a couple hundred feet of us. Two old men were on deck, not even paying attention to us. Just looking out to sea. Their own adventures somewhere on the horizon. Then they disappeared into a thickening bank of fog. If I'd been below deck for thirty seconds, I would've missed them. They would not exist.

My son occasionally asks about his mom, but I remind him we're on vacation, "just the guys."

"You remember that whale we saw this morning?" I say.

"Yeah," he says, looking up at me semi-hopefully.

"Well, that whale is really far from home, but whales always travel in pods, which means there's other whales with him, so, you know, they're always with family no matter what."

"Mom is family."

"Sure. Sure, she is."

"Is Marty family?"

"Sort of, yeah."

"But where's mom?"

"Oh, we'll see her pretty soon probably. We're going to a deep, dark jungle with big volcanoes and all sorts of cool stuff."

My son sighs, looking off into the horizon, his own adventure out there waiting.

"We're going to have lots of fun you and me," I say, telling him the Pacific Ocean of lies.

CUERNAVACA, 1974

MY DAD WAS in volcano country once. Cuernavaca. This was twenty years before the Denver airport. There's a picture of him in an arroyo surrounded by volcanoes with a dozen other men—half of them with big mustaches— around a long table. Everywhere in Cuernavaca back then there were volcanoes and people with big mustaches. The table had a white tablecloth and fine china on it. The men ate things they shot that morning. There was quail, pheasant, wild boar, goose, rabbit, and dove.

My dad did pretty good for a living, but it was more that the dollar went a long way in Mexico back then. Anyway, when they were done eating what they shot they retired to big burlap tents. The kind Teddy Roosevelt would sleep in. They lit pipes and wrote letters to ex-wives and people named Harry. It was autumn, but warm. My dad told me his good friend, Jim Armstrong, brought a bottle of scotch over to his tent to "shoot the

bull." They probably talked about the Zamalek
Disaster or Bebe Buell. The air smelled of tequila
and gunpowder.

Jim Armstrong poured them both a drink and
told him he saw a black quail earlier that morning
when he was off by himself.

"Not just black in the breast or the face," he
told my dad. "All black like a panther."

"Hm," my dad said.

"You ever see anything like that? An all-black
quail?"

My dad told him he hadn't.

"There was something funny about him," my
dad told me years later. "It's hard to explain but
that wasn't Jim Armstrong in my tent that day.
Then he told me he was going to the desert."

"I'm going into the desert now," he told him.

My dad watched Jim Armstrong walk out of
the tent into darkness that smelled like tequila and
gunpowder. The darkness was almost a different
kind of darkness that is hard to explain.

"That was the last time anyone ever saw Jim,"
my dad said.

REINCARNATION

BEFORE WE LEFT the Farallons I wrote a letter and asked Nancy the shark researcher to mail it whenever she reached the mainland.

```
Double Bluff Hill Rd.
Wolf Island, WA 98232

Darling,

I guess it's over, but a part of
me    wishes   it    wasn't.  Things
weren't perfect the last couple
years, but I like to think of us
the way we were in San Francisco
or that time we made love in our
yard while he napped on the big
blue  couch  inside.  Remember  how
you just wore rain boots and that
ski hat?I wish you were here with
us, but I know that isn't possible.
I'm sure you hate me more than ever
now, and are afraid of what might
happen. You should know he misses
```

you, always asking when you will join us, but he is fine.

He is a good boy, isn't he?

I'm not sure what else to say, my love. I hope that doesn't sound strange. I wanted to write you as if I were somehow writing to our past selves, our former love. Also, I guess I want you to know why I'm doing this.

We've reached some point of no return if that makes sense. I can't just sit by and watch him die. There are other things of course, but that I think is the main thing. It is the only thing actually.

I know you will look for us, but it won't be easy, my love. Please tell the police department and the mayor that I'm sorry. Or don't. Forgive me.

Always,
Tom

OPERATION DUNGENESS

IT WAS APRIL when we first found out about our son's rare brain disease and we decided to go to a little seafood place overlooking Padilla Bay. We ordered Dungeness crab and a bottle of white wine. French, maybe. It was sort of in between lunch and dinner, but we went anyway. The thinking being if we were in public it would force us to stop crying and sinking into the floorboards and be an active, normal, crab-eating family for forty-five minutes.

It was a nice day out. Cool, but full of sunshine.

We dipped our crab in butter and watched our son in silence, on the edge of our seats, as if he were the Siege of Leningrad in September of '41. Potential tragedy swirled everywhere. I told my wife I loved her, which was 87.3% true then. This was before the dream of Guatemala and Dr. Haas and kissing that woman on 99th and Madison. This was before monthly MRIs and playing Hot Wheels with the temporarily blind. I took my wife's hand and held it tightly. We watched people pass by the window outside, heading off to their non-brain diseased lives and knew we could never rejoin them. We were now one of *those* families. The ones people talked about in hushed voices over coffee or in a golf cart on the way to the clubhouse for beer and BLTs, reminding each other in the dying purple sunlight how lucky they were, how they can't understand how we do it, how we persevere.

Except later you find out no one perseveres.

No one does it.

We met other parents with kids like ours who seemed like us, but then Facebook later told us their sons and daughters had died on a Tuesday afternoon or a Saturday morning. Their Volvos and Vanagons sat empty, waiting in their driveways forever. Firemen had brought one of them pizza the night before or they watched a baseball game on TV where their favorite player hit a triple. Then their lungs filled up with too much liquid. Or there was something "irreversible."

That's what they got for waiting, I thought.

It is like waking up every day in the middle of a drained-out Mariana Trench and knowing any minute the water and the sharks and the kelp will return.

Two hundred quintillion gallons of salt and blood.

You can almost hear it rumbling in the distance, picking up speed. But I pushed away thoughts of gushing salt and blood. The visions of moms crying alone in their Volvos. I gave warm, buttery kisses to my wife and son. I did this between big, wonderful bites of crab. At one point we smiled about something, but what? What made us eat crab in the first place? What made us smile? Our waiter kept coming over to ask if we wanted the check, but we just looked through him like he was a passing ghost ship. As we ate warm bread, we looked out the window and felt the floorboards softening around us.

TODARODES PACIFICUS

THE COAST GUARD boat is nothing fancy. Aluminum-hulled with an outboard motor, and a .50 caliber machine gun on the bow.

I had been sleeping below deck with my son, so I wasn't ready for them. My Beretta down there somewhere. A hundred ways to strangle a man wearing a life vest suddenly springing to mind.

One of the coasties says he's going to board as the other watches from behind the .50. Below us I can sense all the great whites, and below them the lanternfish, and below them the Greek statues covered in a million barnacles, all of them not giving a shit about what was happening right now.

At this point I realize I don't know where Marty is.

"What's your name?" says the coastie, boarding the Tiffany I with hostile intent.

"Bill," I say real friendly like a gas attendant from 1952. "What's yours?"

"Buddy, we're looking for a kidnapped boy, and have reason to believe he's aboard this vessel."

"Well, that's news to me," I say in the manner of someone's grandpappy, lazing on the back porch after he'd been light-heartedly accused of eating all the rum chiffon pie.

"Are you the only person aboard?" coastie says in a clipped monotone.

That's when I see him.

Fish man.

It's Marty dripping wet with a large, very cheap kitchen knife, creeping up behind the coastie on the .50.

Whether it was the cocaine or all those years in the ocean, he must've been underwater for at least two minutes swimming with that knife. The whole ocean probably watching him like a B-movie. The sperm whales and sea urchins silently cheering him on even though they knew, in the end, he was doomed like the rest of us.

"You're looking at him," I say casually to the coastie like I'm suddenly wearing cut-offs at a picnic somewhere along the banks of the Umpqua River in late August circa 1981.

"I'm checking below deck," says the coastie as he steps aboard.

He goes below deck for about a minute when he comes back up, breathing more heavily now.

His face has changed. Very serious. The cover of *Coast Guard Monthly* come to life.

"Who's the boy down there?" he says raising his gun at me.

I point to his boat where he finds a waterlogged Marty standing behind the .50, the other coastie laid out across the deck like a Japanese Flying Squid after a vicious cornerback blitz.

"You're him, aren't you?" says the coastie, putting down his gun.

"I am," I say.

BISMARCK

"COAST GUARDSMEN DON'T look like Coast Guardsmen when they're tied up in their underwear," says Marty.

Somewhere inside me I want to laugh, but instead I resign myself to watching their Coast Guard boat make panicky last glugs as it sinks into the ocean because Marty knows a thing or two about pumps and scuttling.

After a while we stop ignoring them and go below deck to see what might come out of their mouths.

"You fucking guys," says the redheaded younger coastie, not surprisingly, all things considered.

"Listen," says the older coastie, who's Latino, and not really old—30 maybe. "You don't want to make this worse for yourselves."

"Wow, he really gets us," says Marty, cracking open some Old Fitz.

That's when I realize Marty's wearing one of those old Tyrolean alpine hats with the feather sticking out of it. I don't bother to ask where he got it, or why he's decided to wear it now. Like Schroeder and his Beethoven busts there was probably a closet somewhere full of them.

"The boy," says the older coastie. "Is he alright?"

"Oh, fuck you," says Marty, looking like a pissed off mountain climber from 1931. "This is his fucking dad, not some peeping Snapchat sex enslaver."

"You're the policeman, right?" says the older one to me. "You're a chief of police somewhere up in Washington."

"Was," I say.

"You know they're going to find you, you asshole," says the younger one, struggling against the ropes. "It's only a matter of fucking time, buddy. They're gonna light you up like a Christmas tree!"

"You sure this guy isn't a Marine?" asks Marty. "He sounds kinda scary like maybe he has centerfolds of Fallujah under his mattress."

"What outfit you guys from?" I ask.

"San Pedro," says the older one.

"Long ways," I say.

"You guys are going to Mexico, aren't you?"

"No, we're going to Reno for the rib cook-off western regionals," says Marty, pouring two largeish whiskies.

"You know they got a bounty hunter chasing you cockholes?" says the younger one.

"Cockholes?" says Marty, taking a long thoughtful sip. "Your anger intrigues me."

"Wait. What bounty hunter?" I say.

"Yeah, some private investigator who used to be in the navy," says the older one. "Your—well, someone hired him to find your son."

"You mean my wife?"

"Shit," says Marty. "That's cold."

"What's his name?"

The younger one begins methodically hitting his head against the hull in protest.

"Captain Snow or something," says the older coastie. "Why?"

"Captain Snow?" says Marty. "Are you fucking serious? How did you find us? Was it Nancy?"

"Who?" says the older one.

"You know, the lady from the Farallons."

Both coasties go silent.

"Well, here's to Nancy," says Marty, raising his glass in a toast. "That treasonous slut."

PSALM 23:4

CORTES BANK IS a shallow seamount of sandstone and basalt, ninety-six miles southwest of Los Angeles. It is renowned for producing some of the tallest waves in the world.

We're parked right in the middle of it.

A crystal blue valley with stunning 70-foot cliffs crashing off in the distance.

No islands in sight. Just a couple small boats and jet skis and surfers swimming out towards the walls of water that crash and rise up and crash all over again.

Marty yells out to the surfers that he wants to join them, but they tell him it's too dangerous. Basically, to fuck off.

"Goddamn it," says Marty. "You can't learn anything by being scared."

He puts on his swim trunks and jumps in.

"Where the fuck are you going?" I say, but he can't hear me.

I sigh. Then I make sure the coasties are tied up good and go back topside where my son is watching Marty swim away.

"Is he really going out there?" he says.

"He'll be back," I say, not entirely sure.

I look out at our own private valley, a dusty emerald green at the edges then transforming into shifting molten blues, dark at first, then ultramarine, then Egyptian blue, followed by a burst of intense cobalt around our boat.

"Let's go," I say, giving his head a fatherly rub. "Not way out there. Just into this water here. This might be the most perfect water we'll ever see. Look at it!"

We get in slowly.

Mostly I hold him and we laugh in that nervous way you do when you're in the middle of the ocean. I wonder about hammerheads and white tips. Occasionally we stick our heads underwater. It's clear visibility to about 80 feet. Darting schools of silver mackerel and sunny green surf grass swirling like Nebraska corn fields. A wave, not of fear or elation, but of jealousy comes over me. None of the fish had ever heard of Vein of Galen. Not one sea lion had ever heard of the Dave Matthews Band, or had a future ex-wife hire an ex-naval commander to hunt them

140

down before they could reach the jungles of Guatemala.

I realize the ocean is full of death, but no fear.

I realize this as our legs dangle high above the giant undersea canyon that plummets and stretches out to Tokyo and the graves of a million Malaysian fisherman.

But then I let the jealousy go.

There's too much to think about already so I just let it recede out of me like low tide back in Padilla Bay when all the busted crab traps and goose-barnacled moorings got exposed like old scars.

I lay back into the water and tell my son to do the same.

"Why do we have to?" he asks me in the same voice that greeted needles and MRIs.

"It's ok," I tell him, as the Pacific Ocean sloshes around his little shoulders. "Just follow me."

He struggles at first. The water keeps going into his mouth, or he starts to sink, but then I get him to relax. I tell him to pretend he is the lightest thing on Earth. He starts to get the hang of it. Then we just look up at the clouds together. Big, layered pearly puffs rolling out like a never-ending honeycomb high up in the stratosphere. In the back of my mind I worry about the hammerheads and the white tips, but I don't tell him that. I just hold his hand tightly. I just breathe in and out.

HAYSTACK ROCK

ONE SUMMER ON the Oregon coast near Haystack rock I heard about a good place for bodysurfing, so my wife and I packed some beer and salami sandwiches and got in the car to go see.

When we got there someone said not to swim too close to the point or the locals would slash your tires, so we stayed in the cove. In between rides we wrapped around each other like doting driftwood that had no comprehension about things like dissolving the bonds of matrimony or space polymer embolization.

In the distance, red-hawks we're flying around, which seemed to heighten things, like maybe nature was secretly rooting for us. It was a very clear, very sunny day, which at that point still didn't mean something horrible was about to happen.

Later that evening some locals invited us over to their bonfire. They told us a fourteen-year old girl had been pinned by a log in the surf just down the beach and died that same afternoon. Her whole family was there, but it didn't matter. She died in a swimsuit her mother probably went out to buy for her that spring, never once imagining the broken ribs it would hold together or the drowning it would witness.

"It was just a big stupid log like this," said one of the women, pointing at the thing everyone was sitting on.

INTRODUCTIONS

IN THE MIDDLE of the night the radio flickers to life like the ghost of Pacific past.

"...*(garbled) Tiffany I, over. This is Captain Snow to Tiffany I, over...Do you copy Tiffany I? I know you're out there, fellas. I'm not far behind. Should over-take you in less than a day. Stop now and I'll take you back stateside before the federales get to you...This is Captain Snow to Tiffany I, over...Chief Bell? Is that you? I don't want to take your son chief, but I have a job to do, which entails some future discomfort on your part, I'm afraid. Catch my drift, chief?...This is Captain Snow to Tiffany I, over...*"

I turn off the radio.

"Well, he sounds pleasant," says Marty, pouring us both an Old Fitz.

THE VIETNAM VETS OF MEXICO

MY SON AND I look out at the coast of Baja as Marty moves us into shallower water to finally drop off the half-naked coasties.

"Return to Sender," I tell them, preparing another Old Fitz.

That's when gunfire suddenly erupts off the bow. Just little pops and flashes like we've awoken the paparazzi of the North Pacific. So much for Baja being our tropical mailbox, I think.

"I wish we had that .50!" Marty yells, taking what passes for evasive action in a 1959 diesel trawler.

I go to the mid-cabin to check on my son, but he has on headphones, happily watching TV. I dig out my gun and kiss him on the forehead. When I get back, the half-naked coasties look frightened and embarrassed, like they've been transported to the wrong movie and want to speak to their agents. As Marty hits the gas, I suddenly find myself airborne going in the opposite direction of Tiffany I. I fly past the coasties and the little stove and the little ladder and then I'm outside sliding across the deck, but I somehow don't go directly in the ocean. Instead I keep low against the stern. I empty an entire clip in the general direction of the incoming fire like it's the Mekong Delta in '68 or the Tenderloin in '86.

We get a half-mile or so before we have to drop anchor, smoke billowing from somewhere deep within Tiffany I.

"You whore!" screams Marty.

I grab my son and Marty grabs the Fitz. We wade ashore.

"Let's get behind those rocks," I say.

My son looks flustered, so I give him a big smile. *Nothing to see here, champ!*

We hide behind the rocks and wait.

"Dad, what's happening?" says my son, taking my hand.

"How many bullets do you have?" says Marty.

"Not as many as they do," I say. And when I turn around to think a little about our situation, that's when I see them. Three senior citizens. All of them decked out in face paint and ammo belts, pointing M-16s at our heads.

They say we're their prisoners and take us to "base camp," which is a collection of huts and foxholes hidden behind a grove of palm trees. According to them, their names are Hair-net, Scofield, and Jiffy.

"What the hell are you doing here anyway?" says Hair-net.

So, I tell them about my son's brain trying kill him, and my wife in Palm Springs, and the Coast Guard and the bounty hunter.

No one says anything.

Then Scofield gets up and leaves for a while before returning with a big smile.

"They're fucking coasties in there alright."

Nobody likes the Coast Guard, I think.

The senior citizens finally relax and tell us they're Vietnam vets that have been hiding out ever since they all went AWOL together in '71. They were drug-runners for a while, but now they're retired, living off the land, running old army drills to stay in shape.

"Sorry about all that," says Hair-net. "We've been in this spot for over thirty years and no one's come that close. We thought you were maybe Phoenix Program, or some of George Carver Jr.'s goons."

"I can probably help you fix your boat," says Scofield. "I was a swift boat captain."

Marty and Scofield trudge off down the beach together like a time-warp come to life.

Hair-net tells me there used to be five Vietnam vets in Mexico, but one died of bone cancer in 1980, and another got homesick and went back to Minneapolis-St. Paul to start a bakery.

Jiffy is the least talkative of the Vietnam vets, but after a dinner of fried fish and Acapulco Gold he talks for the first time.

"In Trang Do Duc there was all kinds of mosquitoes," he says. "Like probably five hundred kinds. Some were as big as lug nuts. We had firefights all the time and it was hot and rained almost every day. Mostly I stomped around in the mud in my big green poncho, smoking weed or opium while talking about tripwires and someone's girlfriend back home who was waiting for them in a gingham dress on a farm where the sun sets copper and amethyst. Late at night I would go on patrols looking for zipper-heads, which is what we called the gooks. Mud was everywhere. We hiked through old temples probably full of skeletons and jewels and we kept asking each other for cigarettes and if anyone had 'a bad feeling about this.' When someone said they did we laughed and checked our ammo and snapped at mosquitoes with wet towels like it was a high school locker room where everyone dated cheerleaders and drove Ford Mustangs home on dirt roads."

Hair-net and Scofield laugh as if it's an inside joke of some kind then everybody sort of relaxes and just looks up at the rocketing palms.

"You know, you probably don't have to be down here anymore," I tell them. "It's been a long time."

"Not long enough," says Hair-net. "Not for what we did."

Marty stays up late with the Vietnam vets of Mexico as my son and I drift off to sleep in a hammock near the moonless Pacific.

The next day Scofield helps repair our engine, and they agree to drop the coasties on the nearest highway.

We say our goodbyes and are about to re-board Tiffany I when we see it.

A massive yacht playing "Anchors Aweigh," coming full speed, five-hundred yards down coast.

"Captain Snow," I whisper to the ocean.

The Vietnam vets of Mexico wave us on board and take up defensive positions along the tree-line. The last thing I see of them is Jiffy fixing a bayonet with a big smile on his face.

As Marty pulls away from shore towards the volcanoes of Guatemala, we hear the familiar sounds of machine-gun fire like a living monument to the Vietnam vets of Mexico.

"I liked them," says Marty.

I nod in agreement, watching tracers flit across the waves.

"How about those fireworks?" I say to my boy, mussing his hair.

GHENGIS KHAN

BEFORE LEAVING I gave a letter to Hair-net
to drop in the mail whenever they passed a
mailbox next.

```
Double Bluff Hill Rd.
Wolf Island, WA 98232

Hello darling,

    Remember when we talked about
living abroad for a few years? But
after the diagnosis we never spoke
of it again. Where did you want to
live? I was always curious about
Oslo. Or maybe Hokkaido. All that
good snow and noodle soup. It's too
bad. You would've looked so pretty
in Japan.


    We're very far away now. I wish
you could see him. Such a good boy.
```

He seems bigger to me these days.
I know it's only been a week or so,
but the sea air will do that to
you. Does that give it away? Do you
know where we are? Maybe you do,
but that's ok. We'll be deep in the
jungle soon. Too deep for that
cracked admiral you hired. Yes,
we've met him.

You always make things
interesting don't you, darling?

I'll give him a kiss for you.

Lovingly,
Your future ex

NO CATS

MY SON HAS been complaining of headaches recently and doesn't want to play Hot Wheels.

"How is he?" says Marty, acting fidgety as he lights his one-hundred and twenty-seventh cigarette of the evening.

"I don't know," I say, joining him inside the deckhouse. "Unless you have a CAT scan on board."

"What about this Haas guy? He gonna be there?"

"He'll be there."

Marty looks out at Tiffany I's nose pointed towards the mulberry hued horizon.

"Listen," he says. "I don't know what happens after all this. What happens to me or you or if you're even coming back. I just want you to know you're a good dad. This is the right thing you're doing. I know your wife probably hates your guts and the cops and the FBI are after you, but you should be proud of yourself. I mean I loved my dad, but I don't think the son of a bitch would've done anything half as crazy as this. I don't think he would've taken me across the ocean to hike through some jungle to find some kraut surgeon on the lam. Risk his marriage? His career? His life? Nah, he would've just done whatever they told him to do. Play it safe. Assume the fucking worst. You need guts to actually make up your mind and do something like this."

"Shit, Marty, you must be blind," I say, taking one of his smokes. "This is the most scared out of my wits I've ever been."

FLORIDA STATE SEMINOLES

VOLCANOES . IT SMELLS like volcanoes all the way off the coast of Zihuatanejo and Acapulco. I ask my son if he can smell them, but he just laughs. We are making good time now, and no sign of Snow.

What I notice most is the thing we are doing has become real. It has weight and texture.

I will never see Wolf Island again, I think. Padilla Bay will just be a thing that flashes through the mind like a biological postcard. Cast in the blue bronze of memory and filled with the otters of regret.

On one side of us is Mexico, and on the other side the Pacific. Marty casts a line for dinner as pelicans launch into the troposphere. I watch my son's head against the backdrop of soft green swells, rising like the impatience of fresh hospital sheets. I even admire my son's head for a moment. It's a beautiful head. So much budding greatness and lurking death contained within one tiny skull.

Although his head is actually much bigger than the average boy his age. I can't remember by how much, but it's a medically considerable difference. You can't really tell unless you look for it. You'll notice he can wear my dark blue police chief cowboy hat. You'll notice on occasion it's difficult to pull a shirt over his head. Not a wet turtleneck, but a regular old T-shirt. He never notices though. Or doesn't seem to. Nothing fazes him. They had a special "large" helmet on his T-ball team just for him and no one ever said a word. The barbers, too. He would talk about triceratops or ninjas and they would just smile. They would just go right along and cut the hair on his abnormally large skull like it wasn't filled with too much blood. Like it wasn't secretly trying to kill him. Like he was just four years old and needed a haircut.

I love that beautiful head of his, but I also hate it.

The other day his eyes were hurting so he had to go below deck for a nap.

Marty was down there, too. Out of cocaine and not feeling so great.

That's when I saw the whale shark.

It was just the two of us.

It appeared suddenly from beneath the boat, swimming west. It was like seeing a giant mutant goldfish, or the entire Florida State Seminoles football team gliding just beneath the surface, their gold helmets glinting in the sun.

Freakish yet beautiful.

GUATEMALA

GUATEMALA IS A country in Central America bordered by Mexico, Belize, the Caribbean and the Pacific Ocean. It has an estimated population of 16.6 million people, 8,327 species of poverty, and seventeen pelicans with some form of depression. When you see it you think to yourself, "this is Guatemala." You don't say it out loud. You just think it. You also think about jaguars and volcanoes and other kinds of probably non-depressed pelicans. You think about shitty whisky. You think about hotels where they still wear white jackets. My son's rare diseased brain is in Guatemala, although Guatemala's rare diseased brain population is at present unknown.

"This is Guatemala," I say to my son when we arrive in Guatemala.

PART THREE

EL PAREDON

HERE WE ARE in the waiting room of Guatemala.

I am at a train station in a phone booth overlooking the ocean. The sky is clear and blue except for one massive cloud like one of those wall-sized paintings you find in a nice public library.

I call my wife who is back on Wolf Island.

I want to tell her what is happening, but I don't know how.

"Hello?" she answers.

The feeling (love? something similar?) she had for me before the thing with the diagnosis is somewhere else now, underwater maybe, or floating in the clouds over Machu Picchu, disoriented, lost. You maybe never know when the feeling first goes away, but when it does you can never get it back no matter how good looking you are, or how much money you have tied up in

RV parks in Tennessee, or even how many times you talk to her about Tom Cruise without laughing. You could say, "I want to move to Oslo with you," and she would answer, "On the computer," which will make you wonder whether or not you took life seriously enough. Did you laugh when she suggested bi-weekly family budget meetings? Did you talk about the capital gains tax in a focused, yet casual way at dinner parties that made other people simultaneously fear and respect you?

"Tom?" she says.

I tell her I still love her, but not out loud.

She sighs, and hangs up.

I look over my shoulder to see if anyone is following us, except there's nothing but sky and the trees and maybe a red hawk with a trout in its mouth.

WEDNESDAYS

ONCE YOU SLEPT next to your son in bed wondering how he would die. What hospital room? Would he stop breathing while looking at you? Would his hand sort of grab your hand while looking just over your shoulder at the light or some section of sky out the window? He was born the same way you were except there's too much blood in his head and that means you might not be able to have Thanksgiving together when you're older. It means there's a part of you that nature will exploit.

Everything will be different one day, you think. No Wolf Island. No Guatemala. No ice cream on the boardwalk at dusk in Maui.

The hospital will sound like a forest.

Your loved ones will talk like glaciers.

You will have on a World War II documentary while putting on pants in the late afternoon and then stop in the middle of putting them on.

"This is life," you will say to yourself, eating a half-smooshed avocado as dive-bombing Stukas light up the black-and-white fjord behind you.

NORTH-BY-NORTHEAST

THE THREE OF us are taking a train to Antigua.

It's an old black train with big white numbers on the side. It's the sort of train that shouldn't be alive in these times.

As I drink a cold beer, I look out the window. My son's brain is traveling upriver to spawn like a salmon, and my heart is a freshwater trout. We wriggle in silence. Together we will go build pillow forts in the dark swirling parts of a cold mountain stream just below the tree-line, gurgling. We will lead happy normal lives and have better than average life expectancies. We will have a lovely garden of algae and mud.

"Splooosh," I'll say to him, which in our underwater language roughly translates to, "Go to sleep, my boy."

I continue to look out the window.

Jungle.

Blue sky.

Bird.

Multiple birds.

Dr. Haas is out there somewhere.

I like to travel. The forward motion of it. My wife and I used to travel. We traveled to Mexico mostly and had our honeymoon in Europe. In Greece, we had sex on a ferry in the middle of the Sea of Crete. We smoked French cigarettes. We drank cheap wine on trains at midnight. In Mexico, she wore a green bikini and we ate BLT's and drank Coke with real sugar cane in it. In America, they use corn syrup instead, but obviously it's better with real cane sugar. Also, the bottles are smaller. People are smaller in Mexico, too, but that is unrelated.

The last time we made love in a foreign country was a Sunday. I was making margaritas, preparing to read the international paper about either the Clemson Tigers, or how many people had purportedly just been crushed in a foreign earthquake. She took off her swimsuit and I put down the shaker. Afterwards we took a shower together. I will never shower with her again in this lifetime. In the course of a lifetime people rent more movies about multiple car explosions than have showers with someone.

Someone walks by our sleeper, an elderly, sun-browned man. "Do you know where this train is going?" he asks.

Marty tells the man he is dying of long-term cardiac arrest.

"Probably leg cancer, too," says Marty, looking off into the middle distance in the way a person dying of imaginary leg cancer might.

"Oh, I'm—I'm sorry," says the man, confused, and walks away.

Marty tells me with great sadness he is out of cocaine and orders another beer.

My son is asleep.

I get up and I go to the bar car.

I crawl into a big leather chair to take a nap. When I wake up the woman from 99th and Madison is there.

"Katherine?" I say.

"Don't make any sudden movements," says Katherine. "Some sea captain is at the other end of the bar car and he doesn't seem to like you."

TROUT

INSIDE THE SLEEPER I can smell only Katherine's shampoo, which makes me happy. Wildly happy?

She has on dark blue jeans and a crisp white blouse that shows her throat nicely. She still looks like a 1940's person, but one who lives possibly in Sag Harbor, or somewhere like Sag Harbor. For someone so desperate she looks smart and capable. Like a Roosevelt, but with better teeth. As I look at this attractive Roosevelt-person I realize that I like her even more than I thought.

"Why do you have a gun?" says Katherine.

"How do you know about that?" I say.

"It was falling out of your coat while you were sleeping."

"Did anyone else see?"

"I don't think so."

"Are you sure he doesn't know we're here?"

"The sea captain? No. But he knows you're going to Antigua somehow. He asked if I'd seen two American men with a boy."

"I paid cash and gave the attendant fake names," I say, knowing that probably won't be enough.

"And the gun?"

"I'm a police chief," I say. "Or I used to be. It's sort of complicated."

"I didn't think I'd see you again, Chief Bell."

I like her voice. I like the way she breathes in and out.

"How did you get here?" I ask.

"We flew. My husband, my son and me."

"Your husband?"

"He stayed for a couple days, but then he left. He said he would be back in a day or two, but that isn't true."

"Doesn't believe in witch doctors, huh?"

Katherine smiles. "It's good to see you."

"You too," I say.

"Are you going to Casa Encantada?"

"Yes. I guess that's where we wait."

"How's your son?"

"He's good, how's yours?"

"Good."

We both relax and look out the window at the world rushing by in bright pulses of blue and green. We are alone in her sleeper cabin. Our sons are playing one cabin away while Marty naps. I haven't told him about Snow yet. Not until I have some kind of plan.

"Do you know 'North by Northwest'?" I ask.

"Hitchcock movie?" says Katherine.

"Yeah. This sort of reminds me of that except instead of the CIA or whatever we're being chased by sea captains and exes."

"Where's your wife?"

"She left me, too."

"But not in Guatemala."

"That's true. Guess I'm not sure where she left me exactly."

"But are you glad to be here? I'm glad to finally be here. I think I hate everyone back home."

"Why?"

"They always look scared, but pretend that everything is ok. You ever notice how scared everyone looks?"

"Are you scared?"

"A little."

"Are you hungry?"

"What do you have?"

"Let's order some trout amandine and some Gibsons."

"What's a Gibson?"

"It's like a martini, but has a cocktail onion instead of an olive."

I call the porter and order the trout and the Gibsons for us and chicken with tortillas for Marty and the boys.

I try to kiss her, but she says, "Not right now. I'm too distracted. This whole thing is very distracting."

"Ok," I say.

The porter comes in with two steaming trays.

I pay the porter.

I look both ways down the hall, but I don't see Captain Snow.

"What's this again?" Katherine asks.

"Trout fried with butter and almond shavings."

We eat trout amandine and drink Gibsons like Cary Grant and Eve Saint Marie.

"Do you think Dr. Haas will be there?" asks Katherine, playing with her cocktail onion.

"I hope so," I say.

Katherine looks out the window. "Sometimes it doesn't sound real," she says.

"Nothing sounds real if you think about it," I say.

"Are you scared?"

"Sort of. I used to be more scared because all I was doing was thinking about it and not doing anything. Now I'm doing something at least."

"I like doing something, too," I agree.

I look out the window. In a field two fishermen watch us pass. One of the fishermen has an expression like he wished he were somewhere else—Palm Springs or Sag Harbor in the 1940's. Playing croquet with a martini while watching the sunset from an Adirondack chair. His whole future ahead of him shining like phosphorus. This all happens in the blink of an eye.

LARGE NORWEGIANS PART ONE

IN THE MIDDLE of the night we sneak off the train in the little town of La Democracia.

Just me, my son and Marty again.

We walk through town and buy some sweet bread. It's good bread. We tear off big pieces of it for breakfast as we walk by pastel churches and houses that seem to be smaller than usual, as if the town hadn't yet grown up with the world. Even the trees seem smaller.

"Does this town seem strange to you?" asks Marty, who is now carrying a machete he commandeered from some villager's yard after the news of Captain Snow hot on our trail.

I don't answer him. I'm too tired to answer. And who cares really if it is strange, I think. It's comforting to know there are still strange places out there. But I don't say this. I just continue walking with my son on my shoulders, wearily tearing off hunks of sugary bread like a zombie whose undead mission is to find world-renowned interventional radiologists in a Guatemalan haystack.

We look for a bus station, but we can't find one. It's too small perhaps for the naked eye.

We are giants here.

We could roam the entire countryside in just a few hours, using our big John Wayne-American strides, devouring everyone's bread in sight. We could sleep up in the high mountain jungle, using Mayan temples as beds and jaguars for alarm clocks.

"Why are we not on the train anymore?" asks my son.

"Because we want a little adventure, don't we?" I say. "This way we can see the whole countryside."

My son doesn't answer. He's been rubbing his eyes again, but I don't ask him about it because it will only make things worse.

Marty is on day two or three without cocaine.

As we keep vaguely heading east, I see some farmers in the distance like figures in a model train set. I want to pick them up and move them to the coast so they can jump in the ocean and wash off the mud, smiling gratefully.

But then as we keep walking, the world gradually grows back to normal size. The road turns into the jungle. I spot an electric blue sparrow. Marty spots the largest rodent in the world, which according to him is capable of producing varying purse and shoe sizes.

"They skin them alive then hang them to dry in gambling parlors along the Rio Orto," says Marty.

"How do you know that?" I ask.

"Fuck you," says Marty.

We find a nice-looking stream next to a bodega and decide to rest. I buy two caguamas of beer. Caguama means sea turtle. They are big and cold with beads of sweat already forming on the glass from the heat. I also get some freshly made tamales and we have lunch under a normal-sized tree near some normal-sized Guatemalan cows.

After lunch, we run into two large men with bushy shocks of blonde hair, fly-fishing with two local girls dressed in tight skirts and high heels. The four of them are accompanied by an almost empty bottle of cognac.

"My name is Raid," says one of the men with a thick accent. "He's Tron."

Tron waves. "We're brothers. We're from Norway."

The Norwegians are both easily six-foot-seven, all of their appendages hollowed out and filled with cognac.

"And these are the girls," says Raid like a Viking Vanna White, motioning to the overly made-up girls as if they were a shiny new washer and dryer by Maytag.

I look over to Marty who's frozen in mid-eyebrow raise, more than likely already calculating the rich anecdotal possibilities to be deployed back at The Goose Bottom.

"You're from Norway, huh?" says Marty, looking over the scene as if it were a suspect fender bender.

"To be specific we're from Trondheim," says Raid, heavy traces of cognac on his breath.

"Specifically, yes," nods Tron.

"Is that near Oslo?" I ask.

"Not really," says Raid. "It's a long flight though. Twenty hours. But we come every year anyway for the fishing and a little fun," he says, playfully nudging one of the girls.

"We're professional fly-fishermen," says Tron.

"That's true," adds Raid.

So, we sit down awhile to watch them try all sorts of crazy casts under tree branches and curling behind rocks. One time, Tron sends his fly about two hundred feet downstream with just a flick of his wrist.

But then the Norwegians take a break to open another bottle of cognac, and to see Marty's machete so he lets them look at it.

Tron gives his fly-rod to my son and teaches him how to cast.

"There are big piranha in there," Tron says to my son, his eyes never leaving the water.

"What are piranha?" asks my son.

"They're fish with big sharp teeth," says Tron. "Last week we saw an American catch one and he posed for a photograph with it."

"That was a mistake," says Raid.

"Big mistake," says Tron.

"What happened?" asks my son.

"The fish slipped and bit off his thumb," says Tron.

"Clean off," says Raid, shaking his head. "I think he was from San Francisco."

"No, it was San Jose," says Tron.

We all watch my son practice casting for a moment, wondering about all the thumb-hungry piranha in there. He looks happy, too. Refreshed in a way. The interaction with someone other than Marty and myself. We need to get to the hotel soon, I think. The stories of rendezvousing with his mother are wearing thin. Plus, he looks tired. "Overall children crave routine," I remember my wife reading aloud a passage from one of her parenting magazines. We used to do that Sunday mornings in bed. Read aloud things we found funny or important while reading the paper or some magazine. Maybe some classical music floating in from the living room. Smells of coffee intermingling with the faint sea air seeping in through the cracked window. Sometimes in between articles we would have sex or just hold each other, breathing into each other's hair. This was before 99th and Madison. This was before Palm Springs became a flanking maneuver.

"Why do you have a machete?" Raid asks Marty.

"Why do you have hookers?" asks Marty.

I hold my breath for half a second, but then everyone laughs, even the hookers.

The Norwegians seem friendly, but we tell them we have to continue east so my son gives back their fishing rod, and they give back Marty's machete along with a nine-inch blackthroat they caught earlier in the day.

We thank them and the three of us start out down the road going further into the jungle.

"Are we heading east?" I yell back at the Norwegians, but we're too far to be understood, so the Norwegians just wave back as if he we're saying goodbye one last time, which I realize in a way we are.

THE GUATEMALA OF HOSPITALS

99TH AND MADISON was the Guatemala of hospitals. The O.R. was the jungle and vending machines grew like sweetgum trees. The night sky was vast and star-sprayed with the urgent glow of heart monitors.

Sometimes in the Guatemala of hospitals I felt like I might have a massive heart attack. I would rub my chest to warm it up, to loosen it, to make my trout heart wriggle and flop back to life. If that didn't work, I would pour whisky into a paper cup and drink it down fast like cold medicine.

Before we went to the Guatemala of hospitals my wife and I would lay out what we were taking on the bed, like it was special equipment for some soon-to-be famous exploration. Everything was special down to the socks you wore because those could be the socks you wore the last time you saw him. They might be the socks you wore as you cried in an elevator with other people in it or

181

clutching a vending machine for dear life. You would remember those socks forever.

My son was not afraid of the hospital of Guatemala except when it temporarily blinded him.

Mostly he was bored.

He played Hot Wheels and watched cartoons. He asked why mommy was crying and then ate a little grilled cheese or tried some apple juice.

As we walk through the real Guatemala I often think about the Guatemala of hospitals.

Clearly this Guatemala is the better of the two.

I like the fresh, warm air and the streams and the mountains.

I like walking through it without smooshing avocados into my mouth.

"We are real explorers in the real Guatemala," I say to my son.

THE CAMPGROUND OF
GUATEMALA

THIS IS THE Campground of Guatemala. We will sleep here for the night.

The Campground of Guatemala is surrounded by jaguars, then silver mines, then future rare diseases, then altocumulus clouds, and finally North Korean satellites.

My son is throwing sticks into a stream. Then he throws rocks at the sticks pretending they are enemy warships. I join him and we sink one or two of them with a steady barrage.

"The air force will have to take care of the rest," I tell him.

"Ka-boom!" he says

Besides being a war zone for my son's life, the Campground of Guatemala is a halfway house for cocaine aficionados who happen to also be explorers of the Western Pacific.

Marty curls up inside a giant banana leaf and tells me he feels worse than he's ever felt. More than when he sold Mercedes for a living.

We leave him inside the banana leaf and make a fire. I cook up the fish the Norwegians gave us as my son looks on. Teaching your son things about cooking fish over an open fire is one of the main attractions of the Campground of Guatemala.

"Dad, I'm tired," he says.

"I know," I say.

EL CASTILLO

JUST AS THE sun is about to set my son spots a castle through the trees. At first, I don't believe him, but there it is. All gray stone with a turret and everything.

It turns out to be a nice little hotel with a golf course, so we get a room for the night.

"Do you want dinner in the dining room?" an old man in a worn red server's jacket asks.

"No, in the room's ok," I say.

They bring us steak and some bread and a bottle of wine. We eat in our beds. My son says the steak tastes "super delicious," and for a second, I don't think about death. For a second I wonder if there are certain places in the world death doesn't know about, like this castle, or the bottom of the Mariana Trench, so if you stay there and possibly even live there for the rest of your life, things like massive heart failure or arteriovenous malformations, those things will never find you. I let myself believe this for a little while because it feels good. In the end just feeling good has value somehow. Maybe it doesn't matter if you're honest with yourself or not because honesty and self-awareness are somehow overrated, or don't exist in the way we initially thought they should.

It is pitch black outside our big window facing the golf course.

Marty delicately puts his machete under his pillow.

I look at old books on a shelf and pull out something about the waterfalls of Central America. My son curls up next to me. He carefully traces the waterfalls down to the rocks with his finger.

In the middle of the night I go down to the kitchen for something to eat.

I make toast.

I breathe in and out in the darkness of the castle.

I smell the bread beginning to burn.

Outside the kitchen window I think I see something run by, but I don't go outside to investigate because I'm too tired and a little cold.

After eating the toast, I go outside in my boxers anyway, but there's nothing there.

The next day because we're so tired we decide to stay another night.

Marty and I play a little golf, my son following us and smacking a shot here and there.

On the 16th hole Marty hits it out of the bunker and it goes in which makes him jump up and down wildly like Tom Watson at Pebble Beach in '82.

We order cognacs on the patio overlooking the golf course. Mist from the distant waterfalls leak through the trees like smoke.

Marty swishes the cognac around in his mouth like some kind of vassal, nodding to my son. "This is the life, huh sport?"

"What's the life?"

"To live like this. Not a care in the world."

"Dad, is this the life?"

I tell him it is.

I look at the jungle, bulldozing it in my mind, building a giant mausoleum out of precious Guatemalan metals, looking out over the valley. People like me, a thousand years from now, would lose their golf balls near it and see some kind of plaque that would say something about our journey, about my son, but I'm not sure exactly what.

At night, I get into bed with my son and a cognac and I read about the volcanoes to the east where Dr. Haas is waiting for us.

LARGE NORWEGIANS PART TWO

IN THE MORNING, we find the Norwegians and the hookers in the dining room eating breakfast. We all eat together, laughing about the odds of running into each other. Raid and Tron are drinking cognac already, excited about a good fishing spot nearby.

"We love cognac," Raid says, filling glasses for everyone.

"Yes," Tron says.

"It's like your milk," Raid says.

"We don't really drink milk anymore," I say.

"Fucking A," Raid says.

"Yeah, fucking A," Tron says.

We all drink more cognac.

The Nords ask why we're in the middle of the jungle, and so over the course of a cognac I tell them about my son, Dr. Haas, my wife, Tiffany I, and Captain Snow.

"Sounds like you're looking for the fountain of youth," says Raid, placing one of the hookers on his lap as he looks thoughtfully at my son's head. "We are looking for something, too, you see."

"What are you looking for?" asks Marty, still not looking a hundred percent.

"The piranha-otter."

"What the hell is that?"

"No one's sure because no one's seen it," says Tron.

"That's not entirely true, Tron," says Raid. "It was sighted quite frequently by gauchos around the turn of the 20th century."

"How big is it?" asks my son, clearly happy to see the foursome again.

"About as big as a regular otter," says Raid.

"But with teeth like daggers," says Tron.

"Yes, but with teeth like daggers," agrees Raid.

Marty and I can't tell if they're pulling our legs, but the Nords gather their fishing equipment and the hookers and we take two Land Rovers out past the golf course to go fishing for the dreaded piranha-otter. Sitting next to Marty, I suddenly realize he looks ecstatic for the first time in days.

"You look better," I say.

"Yes," says Marty, bouncing happily in his seat. "Raid apparently likes cocaine second only to cognac."

"Of course," I say.

Finally, the SUVs stop at a nice-looking bend in the river. There's a coppery sandbar and tempting still pools with slow swirls and buggy gurgles.

The hookers have on bikinis now. The tall one with the biggest fake breasts has on a sensible blue bikini sporting lacy ruffles along her sun-ambered pelvis. The shorter one with the medium-sized fake breasts has on a bright yellow number that matches her peroxide ponytail. Apparently one of them spotted an alligator the other day, which explains why they carefully set up their towels on the roof of the car.

"Do you have any hobbies?" asks Raid.

"I don't think so," I say, almost surprised at the existence of small talk again.

"Driving sports cars is nice," offers Tron, fumbling with his rod.

"My twin sisters clog," says Raid. "They're what you call cloggers. They co-wrote two clogging self-published memoirs. *It Takes Two to Clog* and *Clogging All the Way to the Bank*. Although I suppose it isn't a hobby since they were world-ranked at one time. Not overly pretty women. Heavy thighs. Stage Four bush."

All of a sudden, I feel too drunk.

I put down my fishing rod and watch the hookers who are now sun tanning while sharing a joint.

Tron makes a long cast to the far side of the river.

"Some people believe piranhas are mystical creatures like gods or werewolves," he says, pouring more cognac down his throat.

"A friend of mine got his heart broken by a piranha," says Raid.

The hookers sometimes laugh at them or move their shoulders to the music blaring from the car speakers, their giant fake boobs jostling in the sunlight for some unknown vantage point.

"I sense the piranha want to tell me something," says Tron.

"I sense the piranha want to tell me to invest my money in a more mature and realistic way," says Raid.

"I sense the piranha want to tell me to dress my hooker like a piranha then marry her and have little piranhas," says Tron.

After fishing for the dreaded piranha-otter we drive back to the hotel and fall asleep without dinner.

The next day we get up and leave before the Norwegians and the hookers wake up. Sometimes it's better not to say goodbye.

I HONK FOR BOOBS

WALKING THROUGH THE town of Yepocapa I suddenly wish I were someone else. Someone who didn't have a species of heart from the *Oncorhynchus clarkii* family. Someone whose son wouldn't die, but instead grow old and have dinner parties above the tree-line in the moonlight, laughing. And when I got too old for dinner parties above the tree-line, we could watch golf together. Then later at night by myself I would stare up at the ceiling, remembering everything we had done together, like water rafting in Idaho, or watching his future wife laugh as he made some off-color joke while grilling steaks. Except human history will go on without us. No one will remember. We haven't discovered anything or gone fast enough on the Bonneville Salt Flats or accumulated enough real estate or saved enough child soldiers from Nigeria. Is it impossible to be happy knowing that you and everyone you know, even Tom Cruise, will be one day be staring at their ceilings in the darkness, weighing ninety-six pounds with the Golf Channel on full volume, smelling a little bit like cat food and ointment, wearing a foam trucker hat that says "I honk for boobs," because one of the hospice nurses was trying to be funny, and then semi-deeply breathing in, then out, then in, then out, then some kind of quiet gurgle?

OUR LADY OF THE GRASS COURT

WALKING ALONG WE see a white monastery on a hill like a cloud that just needed to take a break for a minute.

Then it starts to rain so we run up to the monastery to wait out the storm. Except over the rain we hear something else. A mystery-sound. The soft springy pong of something being hit followed by little grunts, and groans. As we get closer the sounds get louder.

Then we open the big wooden door.

Inside there are no pews, or statues or altars. Instead there are only three simultaneous mixed-doubles tennis matches being played under the massive wrought-iron chandeliers and vaulted roof.

Men and women—all of them wearing ghostly white robes—squeak back and forth in their sneakers like monastic Bjorn Borgs. There's even a little grandstand full of others in white robes looking on in silence. Other than the grunts and groans no one says a word. No "Good shot!" No "Deuce!"

I say hello to one of the monks retrieving a loose ball, but he doesn't answer.

"What the hell kinda place is this?" says Marty.

Someone taps me on my shoulder, and I turn to find an older monk who sticks out in his brown robe.

"Follow me," says the monk in the brown robe.

We follow him outside to a little covered bell tower where we can see the monastery grounds are entirely covered with more tennis courts, grass, clay, you name it. People in white robes are still playing in the rain when the monk rings the bell and they immediately begin to cover the courts, then scatter inside.

"What is this?" I say.

"It's a home for certain people looking for simplicity in their life," says the monk. "They take up tennis and make tennis their life so there's no room for drugs or alcohol or sex or gambling. They play tennis until they forget why they came."

"How long does it take?" I ask.

"Depends. Some people are here for a few months. Most have been here for years."

"And why not," says Marty, gesturing out at the courts like a resort infomercial come to life. "But what about you, monsignor, have you forgotten?"

"I have," says the monk.

We go back inside where the monk offers us tea.

We drink the tea and look around at the place. A few monks are tightening the nets, but otherwise absolute stillness like a low-pressure area around the equator. It's so quiet that Marty forgets to mouth off. He just watches in silence, monastically sipping his tea.

The monk offers to take us around, but I stay to watch my son fall asleep on a wooden bench as rain gently baptizes the jungle outside. Marty goes with him. Following with teacup in hand as if caught in a tractor beam of tranquility.

I watch my boy sleep. He seems peaceful, which is like camouflage for the thing trying to kill him. I want to get on my knees and pray to this little boy. I want him to be ok. Someday he will need to know things only I can teach him. Like the difference between Burgundy and Bordeaux. The significance of George Brett. Or how I fell in love with his mother.

We stay until the rain lets up, and then we're on our way.

"What did you think of that fucking loony bin?" asks Marty, as he does a bump mid-stride, beginning to remember himself. "How do you play tennis until you forget something?"

"Let's just get to Antigua," I say, looking up at the volcanoes rising up on either side of us like the Sphynx Gates.

"What about this Snow guy?" says Marty. "He's probably still looking for us. He might even have a couple hired goons with him."

"It's a big town," I say. "We'll pay with cash and lay low at the hotel until Haas' people come for us."

"Are we there yet?" asks my son, who I can tell is beginning to hate the jungle and distrust his father.

"Just up the road," I say. "Can you see it?"

ANTIGUA

ANTIGUA IS A small city in the central highlands of Guatemala. It is well-known for its Spanish Baroque architecture and is surrounded by volcanoes, tennis monks, and fly-fishing hookers.

Endovascular surgery dominates the horizon of Antigua, sometimes at altitudes of up to 13,000 feet.

Many dreams of foreign origin can be found here:

The white nun orchid

Austrian interventional radiologists

Sea captains paid by future ex-wives to hunt down their loved ones like dogs

Historically, there is nothing like Antigua.

People drink strong coffee and look at old buildings in large groups. They often think to themselves, "How am I changing my life? What place do you go to make everything like it never was?"

People die in Antigua, but they also swim with little turquoise and yellow fish in Lake Atitlan and feel their cheeks get hot in the summer sun.

Did I mention volcanoes?

THE HAAS HOTEL

SIMON HAAS, M.D. is Director of the Pediatric Cerebrovascular Program at Rudolfinerhaus. Dr. Haas was born in Amstetten in 1948 and graduated from the University of Vienna in 1971. From 1973 to 1976, he did his residency in Diagnostic Radiology at the Federal Hospital of Salzburg, where he started the field of what is now recognized as "Interventional Radiology", or "Endovascular Surgery".

This is the beginning of an article in an old medical journal I found. That was three years ago, not long after almost sinking into the floorboards.

The cover is mint green with dense white type. It looks like something you might need for obscure tax codes or launching a tactical nuclear strike. There is a picture of Dr. Haas on the inside. He had sideburns back then. Young and serious. The caption reads, "Simon Haas, M.D.," which could be a hit TV show if the subject matter weren't so boring and sad and full of hospital cafeteria food. Near the end of the article Dr. Haas speaks from December 1990:

"With some of these new procedures, we're treating children who used to die. Now we can do something that's never been done before."

I read this part over and over. It's like Tennyson. I've read it maybe two or three hundred times. It's my favorite part.

I order a whisky.

I'm at the bar of the Casa Encantada.

The whisky is a whisky I've never heard of, called Black Pheasant, and has a picture of a black pheasant on it.

I take my drink and look around the hotel a little. Dusty old colonial, but nice. On one wall in the grand lobby there are ancient black and white photographs of people doing some sort of dance that was popular back in those days like war bonds or toys made from real metal.

Walking around I begin feeling like an old thing, too.

Old people order drinks and wander through hotel lobbies. They think about the fact that their lives are basically over except for maybe a few more drinks at different bars and maybe someone surprises them one more time by laughing differently or developing some facial tic they've never seen before and then they stop breathing for good. That's pretty much all you can hope for.

I go back to the bar and order dinner, a steak, medium-rare.

Someone taps me on my shoulder, and I turn to find Katherine. She sits next to me and orders a Gibson.

"I'm hooked on these things now," she says, looking at me with her green eyes. "Where's your son and that friend of yours?"

I tell her they're upstairs sleeping, but I can't sleep for some reason so I'm here instead.

"You're lucky to have a friend with you, a partner," she says.

As I eat my steak, we talk about Dr. Haas and Captain Snow, who apparently got off one stop before Antigua with another man, someone Guatemalan.

"He's probably making sure we're not staying outside the city," I say. "That would've been smarter."

"Well, not in this case," says Katherine.

"That's true," I say. "Might actually buy us some time."

Katherine tells me there are other people at the hotel waiting the same way we are. Maybe three or four other families. One family went up with Dr. Yomiko two weeks ago, but they never came back. No one heard anything about them, or how the surgery went, or if they even made it.

"Some people think they could've been killed by bandits, or fallen off a cliff somewhere," says Katherine. "Lots of rumors going around. And lots of drinking. A fight broke out last night between two mothers, then their husbands got into it. One woman I talked to said she and her husband were thinking about venturing out to find Haas on their own. It's crazy. Like the hotel is one big waiting room set to explode at any minute."

I ask if she's seen Dr. Yomiko, but she says Yomiko only comes for the families in the middle of the night, and no one knows who's next.

"It doesn't seem to matter how long you've been here," says Katherine, polishing off her Gibson. "They have some other system, or it's totally random. I don't know really. It's so good to see you though."

I watch her eat her cocktail onion mid-sigh.

We order two more drinks and sit in front of the giant fireplace.

"If we were married would you ever divorce me even if I was just being myself?" I say.

"Depends," says Katherine.

"On what?"

"On what 'being yourself' entails."

205

"Nobody knows what that is, *being yourself*."

"I think it means being honest about what you feel inside at a specific moment in time."

"What if inside you feel like a freshwater fish?"

Katherine smiles. "Sometimes you're not very serious for a police chief," she says.

After we finish our drinks we go upstairs.

"I have adjoining rooms so we won't wake my son," says Katherine as she takes off everything but a white bra and yellow, low-cut panties.

I take off everything, but my boxers.

We are on opposite sides of the room.

Outside the window the jungle is pitch-black like a vast nighttime closet.

The dreaded piranha-otter is out there.

Somewhere Captain Snow is looking for us.

Katherine spots my massive hard on poking out the bottom of my boxers. She laughs. Then she turns off the light and goes to where I am standing.

"Do you like huckleberries?" she asks me in the dark.

"I love all berries," I say.

"I make huckleberry jam in the summer. It's not very good though."

"I'd love to try your mediocre jam sometime."

I put my hand on her waist, which makes her stomach muscles flutter in the darkness. We are both breathing heavy. We kiss for a little while, rubbing against each other in the darkness like sexual Braille. Afterwards we both stretch out on the bed, looking at the ceiling, listening to our heartbeats, and the train rumbling in the distance further east to the Caribbean.

ST. PAUL, MINNESOTA

WE'RE OUT ON the hotel terrace looking at volcanoes the way birdwatchers watch lava-filled condors.

Boys in the swimming pool. Hot, shining jungle everywhere.

"I think he's on that one," says Katherine, pointing at a big volcano to the south. "Which one do you think?"

I tell her I don't feel like guessing. The volcanoes suddenly remind me of death. Like Hans Steiniger tripping over his beard for the last time. Or actor Vic Morrow's head being sliced off by an out of control helicopter. My life is an out of control helicopter, I think.

My heart bubbles and glistens like a cutthroat.

I decide to go up to the room and take a nap.

I have a dream about Katherine. In the dream, we are on a plane to St. Paul, Minnesota, which I think is maybe the most perfect name for a place in all the world.

During the descent, we suddenly take a fairly steep dive, and the entire top of the airplane just sort of rips off its hinges, rising "*Sss-pop!*" backwards in one big banana peel of sun-flashing aluminum. I grab Katherine's hand. She has on a sleeveless white cotton number, which makes her look even more attractive than usual. For some reason, in my dream it is the 4th of July, or maybe the 5th of July. I feel like it is the 4th of July, though.

There is a man with a beard sitting next to me. He is the most upset of anyone.

"We are doomed, man! This whole plane is going down and we are fucking doomed!"

"Look at me," I tell the bearded man in my dream.

The bearded man looks at me with grave seriousness.

I then proceed to explain to him at the exact moment before we're about to crash to jump up in the air.

"Jesus!" says the bearded man.

Katherine snorts out her nose because some people have that thing where they snort out their nose in ridiculous situations.

Out the window I see a frigid pond below most likely laughing at the idea of us jumping up in the air upon impact. Secretly, I hope there will be hunters down there, or at least some boy scouts fishing for trout who would later be held for questioning by the authorities, forced to give impromptu news conferences to the international news media, and with all the hot lights and electrical wires and generators they would ask them one by one what they saw "in their own words" and then they would have to tell them how they saw three people in the peeled back jetliner jump up from their seats just at the point of impact.

"How about that?" I say to Katherine, who isn't snorting anymore, the pond fast-approaching out the window. "Will you remember when I say goodbye to you?"

THE LAST LETTER

Double Bluff Hill Rd.
Wolf Island, WA 98232

Hi darling,

    I saw your friend Snow on the train the other day. We didn't get to chat, but he seems very serious. Remember when we weren't serious, and didn't hire deranged sea captains to find one another? I miss those days.

    Someone once said you don't have to wait to realize the good old days. I think it was Ziggy Marley. I typically agree with any of the Marleys, but I don't think that was necessarily true for me. I always thought things would keep getting better somehow. Did you ever feel that way?

Marty isn't looking so hot these days, but then I know you never really cared for him. I get it. He's difficult as hell, but you can't say he doesn't go the distance. More than we can say, I guess.

We've done quite a bit since we saw you. Your son swam in the middle of the Pacific. We met some nice Norwegians who taught him how to fly fish. We also met some tennis-playing monks.

Very hot and sunny here by the way. It's so hot I woke up in the middle of the night recently and thought of you. How I last saw you. I keep thinking it was raining when we left, but I don't think it was actually. Is it raining there now? Or has it stopped?

That's about it I guess. Take care of yourself.

Climactically,

Tom

THE PATIENTS OF GUATEMALA

THE PATIENTS OF Guatemala are from all over. There are the Patels from Bangladesh who have an infant son. The Schneiders from Pittsburgh with a two-year old girl. The Pooles from Devonshire have a thirteen-year old boy with glasses thick as headlamps. Then there are the Chens from Shanghai. Their three-year old daughter had to go to the hospital one night because of a rupture. I don't remember her name. I only remember Mr. Chen yelling at the bar in tears as they rushed his daughter into an ambulance.

"They fucking take too long!" he screamed in passable English at myself, Katherine and Mr. Schneider. I don't know where the others were.

"What happen when happens to you?" he yelled. "You sit at bar? You sit at bar while your child dying?"

Then he left and we heard the sirens bounce off the volcanoes and the Antiguan night sky.

"Jesus," said Mr. Schneider from Pittsburgh after Chen had left.

I remember the first time I saw Mr. Schneider.

It was by the pool while I watched my son practice holding his breath in the shallow end. Schneider looked me up and down from across the pool, got up, walked over, and sat down next to me.

"I'll tell what you what's happening," he said, looking out at the jaguar-filled valley beyond the hotel. "This Dr. Haas is fucking with us. I think they're probably two or three hotels just like this one packed with families like you and me, that Chen guy, all with our sacks of funny money. Think about it. Twenty-five thousand a pop. Four or five families per hotel. Turn over every month. That's over 4 million a year, tax free. There's no fucking overhead in the jungle."

Schneider was a dentist. He usually wore different colored golf shirts with the bright metallic sheen of a mackerel.

"And who's this fucking Yomiko character?" he said. "She just shows up like the tooth fairy and whisks you off to some surgical fairytale land? Fuck her. We've been here over two weeks now. My wife's about to lose it. I've been drinking like a fish. You have a wife?"

"I don't think so anymore."

"Well, it's a fucking miracle anyone stays married through this shit. You meet in college. You go to San Miguel de Allende for your honeymoon to see the fucking cobblestones. You buy the house in Moreland Hills with a south-facing hot tub. Then wham! Your kid has a rare brain disease that might kill her before she can say her first words."

Schneider lit up a cigarette and looked over at me for the first time since he sat down. "How's he doing anyway? Your kid."

"He's ok," I said. "His eyes bother him sometimes, but he's been pretty good."

"How many surgeries?"

"Six."

"Wow. We're at three. I thought that was bad. You have any complications or anything?"

"Yeah. You?"

"Yeah."

"So, you're friends with that Karen."

"Katherine."

"She has that nice boy. You both have beautiful little boys. Everybody looks so healthy, you know? But..."

A waiter came by, but neither of us looked at him. Schneider took a couple drags from his cigarette. The waiter finally walked away, sensing tragedy like a collie from the '40s senses fire.

"I guess you heard about the McCormicks," said Schneider. "That Scottish family or Irish. I can't fucking remember. Anyway, they left a couple weeks ago and no one heard. My wife is wondering if they got robbed, like maybe it's all a scam, but I don't know. This place is crawling with criminals. Could just be they got robbed by anyone. Maybe that fucking Yomiko got it, too. I don't know. We're thinking of hiring a police escort. You can do that. If you're going somewhere outside the city known for robberies they'll get you a cop or two to go along."

"But I thought Yomiko came in the middle of the night, unannounced?"

"Yeah, I think we'd have to get them on call. You know, waiting for us."

"Have you talked to them?"

"The cops? Not yet. I guess we also feel a little weird. You know, like maybe what we're doing is illegal somehow. Have you thought about that? Or have you heard? That maybe he's on the run from the authorities or something?"

"I think his license was just pulled somewhere overseas."

"Yeah. Yeah, that's what I heard, too. So, what do you think?"

"About what?"

"I mean, if this Yomiko knocks on your door at three in the morning are you going through with it?"

"Yeah."

"Yeah, us, too. I mean—I don't think there's an option, right?"

A few nights after that I had drinks with Schneider and Katherine when Chen screamed at us. The night after that I looked for Schneider at the bar, but he wasn't there. The next night I looked for him again, but there was no sign of him. On the third night, I ran into Mrs. Poole the Englishwoman, who was grabbing two whiskies and some BLTs to go at the bar. She told me they were gone. As she said it, I noticed her eyes seemed dead. They were black like the water in the deepest part of the Tonga Trench.

"No one's seen them since day after last," she said.

"You think they saw Haas," I said.

"Who bloody knows," she said, and left with her whiskies and BLTs.

After dinner, I took my son to our room and put him to bed and then I cried in the bathroom so he couldn't hear me. I cried into a little towel with the hotel logo on it. When I was done, I went back into the room and slept next to my son the way my wife used to. I think about her all the time even though we're divorced in the future. I think about everything really.

AND DARKNESS CREPT OVER THE LAND FROM THE EAST

ONE NIGHT KATHERINE comes to my room in a panic.

"I think he has sunset eyes," she says.

Sunset eyes are something in infants and young children when their brains slowly try to push their eyes out of their sockets from intracranial pressure.

On the train ride to New York my wife and I were constantly looking for sunset eyes, thinking we saw it happening every ten miles, living a sort of eternal heart-attack. We were scared out of our wits, reduced to dumb animals that could hear and sense everything around us, but effect nothing. We were like field mice that had found God in the ultrasonic. The coffee being poured. Every word of every conversation around us. The trees and tunnels all around us amplifying in black blurs. We kept watching, but his eyes never turned.

"Are you sure?" I ask Katherine, trying not to wake my son.

"Jesus, I think so," she says. "Jesus."

I fix her a drink and try to calm her down.

"Can you look at him?" she says gulping down some of her whisky. "I don't know what to think. Maybe I'm seeing things."

"Is he sleeping?"

She nods, drinking down some more.

"Let's not wake him if he's sleeping."

"But I thought you weren't supposed to let them sleep if they get it."

I sigh and agree to come over and look at him.

She turns on the lights and I go to his bed. I try to gently open one of his eyes without waking him, but he wakes up anyway.

"Mom?" he says, looking at me, drowsily.

I look at his eyes, but it's hard to tell. Sunset eyes can be tricky.

"It could be that he's just tired," I tell her, wanting it to be true.

She turns out the light and kisses him goodnight. We go back outside the room and she looks at the carpet in the hall for a moment, considering it like some polypropylene oracle.

"Fuck," she says to the all-knowing carpet.

ACHILLES

BENEATH ALL THE promise and goodwill of the volcanoes Marty has hit rock bottom. He doesn't come out of the room for three days.

Sometimes he comes out from under the covers to watch TV, but there are only three channels and two of them are always very loud gameshows. He makes a sort of whimper at the TV then slowly submerges back beneath the cotton whitecaps.

One day I'm summoned to the dining room. It looks like an insane asylum had lunch with a gas explosion.

The hotel manager tells me it was Marty. Apparently, he tore through the place in the middle of dinner like someone who should be shot on sight. It took four people to bring him down. Luckily a doctor was there and stuffed him with sedatives.

I let him sleep through the next day.

Later that evening I find Marty in our room showered and dressed. His hair is combed for the first time in weeks. He looks like a time-share commercial come to life. He tells me the other night he found some coke off some German tourists and did too much. Then he tells me he is leaving. To go back to the tennis monastery for help.

"I'm tired," he says. "Every day I wake up thinking about how much I need or don't need. Sometimes I think I'm going to die. That's no way to wake up. But I got you both down here, right? We made it."

"Of course, we did," I say.

"And now your son is going to be better, isn't he?"

"Yes sir."

"And then I'll get better too, and we'll go home together like brand new. All of us."

"You've done everything."

Marty looks out the window of Guatemala and takes a deep breath.

"I'm actually looking forward to it, Tom," he says. "I'd like a quieter mind, you know? I'd like to write poetry about the goblin shark, maybe work on my backhand a little."

He gets up.

"Did you say goodbye to him?" I ask.

"You do it for me, ok?" he says. "I think you'd say it better."

He gives me a hug like it's the last hug we'll ever have in this world.

Then he walks out the door.

I almost say something, but then I just let it happen.

I listen to his shoes down the stairs until I can't hear them anymore.

A VISITOR

I AM DREAMING of Marty hitting a baseline screamer in his snowy tunic when I wake to a knock at the door.

"Katherine?" I call out.

"Dr. Yomiko," says the voice behind the door. "May I come in."

I let her in and close the door to my son's room so he doesn't wake up.

"How is he doing?" asks Yomiko.

"He's ok, I think."

I ask if she wants anything to drink, but Yomiko declines. She says she hates to wake my son in the middle of the night like this, but that we need to leave soon if we are to make it to Haas before sunrise. After that she fears there will be more climbers on the volcano and that she doesn't want to attract unwanted attention.

"You have a lot of money on you, Chief Bell, and we would very much like to keep it that way," she says. "That, and we prefer to keep our location a secret. You understand. We'll have a police escort up part of the way, then it'll just be us. Oh, and you must sign this."

Yomiko takes a document from the inside pocket of her jacket and hands it to me with a pen.

"What is it?"

"Just an agreement. That you won't divulge our location among other things. Don't worry. Everyone signs it."

I sign it without reading it.

"Are we ready then?" says Yomiko.

I almost blurt "Ok, let's go," but something about Katherine and her kid nags at me.

"Is there any way that Katherine and her boy can go with us, too?" I ask. "He doesn't seem well."

"I'm afraid we only do one patient at a time," says Yomiko.

"When is she due to go up?"

"Katherine? I can't really say, but perhaps no more than a week or so."

I tell Yomiko that she should knock on Katherine's door. I tell him my son and I can wait a little longer.

Yomiko looks at me for a second like maybe I am a goblin shark only disguised as man whose son's brain is trying to kill him.

"In almost ten years, I've never heard anyone give up their spot, and I doubt Dr. Haas has either," she says. "Some children have become too ill to make the trip, but that's different altogether. Anyway, I suppose you have your reasons."

When she says this, I almost change my mind. I can feel myself holding something inside that wants to scream and take it all back and run my son up the volcano to be saved, but instead I don't say anything as Yomiko opens the door.

"Goodnight, Chief Bell," says Yomiko.

"Goodnight," I say.

CHARLIE THE TUNA

ONE MORNING LONG ago I woke up and it was Christmas morning. Except it was May. And instead of a blanket of snow the whole town was covered in ash.

That was my first experience with a volcano.

St. Helens, 1980.

It killed a few dozen people, and probably more than fifty thousand fish. It was a fish massacre. It was their Somme. Their Gettysburg. But that was far away somewhere locked inside our TV and hidden in the newspaper ink. In my neighborhood, it was gray and quiet like a granite monument to the greatest sacrifice since the Starkist bloodbath of '61.

Years later I climbed a dead volcano. Or dormant, as they say. Its lava was way down there somewhere just waiting for defibrillation. I had a peanut butter and honey sandwich on top of it, right near its icy smokestack that had been there since Paleolithic Europe. This was before my wife and my son. This was before the brain massacres of Guatemala.

Have you ever seen a volcano up close? They don't look like anything special, but they have great potential like that big-boned girl in your niece's soccer game, or an ex-Navy Seal with a sack of fertilizer.

Now I'm surrounded by volcanoes . All of them living and breathing.

I think about Katherine up on her volcano as I read the note she left for me at the front desk.

```
Dear Tom,
     We'll be at the Hotel Alvear
when we return. Three or four days
after recovery. We're not supposed
to be at this hotel anymore for you
know why. Wish us luck!
                    I love you,
                              K
```

We haven't used the word love before. I like that she used it. It feels good to read it. Just as I pour another cup of coffee and get ready to read it again Mrs. Poole knocks on my door to tell me Katherine is in the hospital.

As my head turns into a white fuzzy TV screen, I manage to tell Mrs. Poole to stay with my son.

I run a few blocks up the street, realizing this is my first time outside the hotel in days. Weeks?

When I get to the hospital, they tell me they've stopped the bleeding. She was stabbed at the foot of Volcán de Agua, which means Water Volcano in English. Dr. Yomiko was shot through the throat and died in the ambulance. Katherine's son is ok, but they're monitoring him for hydrocephalus.

I ask if she's going to be ok like in a movie, except this movie stars a goblin shark posing as an ex-chief of police who bravely explores the outer reaches of brain disease and future divorce.

That night Katherine comes to and tells me the police escort stole all her money and shot Yomiko.

"It was two other guys in masks, but you could tell they worked together," she says with oxygen tubes in her nose. "After they shot Yomiko they were going to kill me, but one of the cops said something in Spanish and they stopped. It was the way he said it. Very calm. Like he was in charge of the whole thing."

I kiss her on the forehead and tell her to sleep.

I walk out of the hospital feeling something.

It's something I haven't felt since when I was chief of police.

HAPPY HOUR

I ORDER A drink at the hotel bar. One drink and then I'll get my gun and find the dirty cops and Katherine's money. Just like that everything will be the way it was. Except for Yomiko. And did that mean Haas might leave? Maybe he doesn't know yet. Or he's already gone. I try not to think about it. It's late now. Soft piano floating through the halls like pale, languid sting rays of sound.

I scoop up a little nut mix out of the silver bowl, realizing I haven't eaten all day. I eat the whole bowl of nut mix just as my drink arrives. I take a good long drink and put my empty glass down when I see something in the mirror behind the bar. Two men are now sitting on either side of me. One of them is a big villager in one of those blazers they give you at the door. The other looks like a sea captain.

I can feel my trout heart writhe and jiggle.

"That was weird," says the sea captain, pushing back a frayed USS Maryland ball cap.

"You know how you think something's going to be extremely difficult, but then for some reason it turns out to be really easy?"

I think about my gun in the suitcase upstairs. Just casually waiting there. Like someone had called it about a league-wide rain-out for armed and dangerous sea captains.

"Oh, where are my manners? I'm Captain Snow and this chap next to you is Garcia. Say hi, Garcia."

Garcia doesn't say anything.

"And just in case you decide to do something questionable you can see your boy is just right over there with my other friend, Lopez."

I turn around and see my son at a table in the lounge next to another large Guatemalan who has ordered him ice cream. My son waves to me innocently. He thinks we're on vacation. His mother will be here soon. To see the ancient temples and museums together.

"What do you want to drink?" asks Snow.

"Whisky," I say.

"Two Saratogas," he tells the bartender. "Whisky, brandy, vermouth and bitters with cracked ice. Stir, then strain into a chilled cocktail coupe with a lemon twist over the top. Chop, chop."

Snow shakes his head as the bartender makes the drinks.

"You know," he says, "this hotel for some reason was the last on my list. I thought it was too nice for you. Big mistake on my part. Anyway, Garcia here was the one that saw you running around outside like a chicken with its head cut off. To see your new girlfriend in the hospital as it were. By the way, I'm sure your wife will be anxious to hear how Katherine is doing."

The bartender clicks two sawed-off goblets on the marble bar top.

"To us," says Snow, raising his drink to no one.

Snow takes a sip and looks around. "Where's your friend, anyway? The cokehead with the fishing boat. He die of an overdose or something?"

I tell him Marty already left.

"That's too bad," says Snow. "Always good to have a wingman in these kinds of situations. Don't you think so, Garcia?"

But Garcia just sits there like a statue on Easter Island.

"Well, I guess we should get down to business," says Snow, as I feel something being pressed into my ribs.

"That's my pistol," says Snow. "I know you're partial to Beretta, but I've always been more of a Sig Sauer kind of guy."

"So, you're going to shoot me in a bar full of people?" I ask.

"I don't know. Do you think that would cause a scene?"

I shrug. "Your call."

"What do you think death is, chief? In your mind do you go to heaven, or is it more along the lines of no longer existing in a way we can fathom in this so-called dimension?"

"___"

Snow continues, "Schopenhauer says only small and limited minds fear death. That individuality ceases with death, but the essence of being is indestructible and remains part of the cosmic process."

"You sound like a fucking idiot," I say.

"You think time is objective and real?"

I begin weighing my chances with a goblet to Snow's temple before trying my luck with Garcia.

Then I think about my son.

We should've shared a six-pack of Coke in a cold stream surrounded by a dam made of sticks and bark. Watched eagles atop carbonized trees. Sharing beans. Sharing part of a cigar. Talk about baseball. We should've camped every weekend instead of once or twice a year. We should've acted like the world is some big cruise liner already half-submerged. But life is more boring than that. You buy a new tie. You find out how far it is to the nearest H&R Block. Somehow you forget there's a time limit and then everything has slipped away, the water calm and silent again, acting as if you were never there in the first place.

"Ok, we're going to walk out of here very placid-like," says Snow. "I'm taking your boy back home to his mother, and Garcia and Lopez here are going to take you to their village for a while. Who knows what will happen there. Isn't that right, Garcia?"

This time Garcia answers. "Boss?" he says.

I look up at the mirror behind the bar and see Raid and Tron are now sitting on either side of Snow and Garcia. They have snifters of cognac and two large machetes with them. Tron has his machete pointed at the ribs of Garcia, and Raid runs his giant blade between Snow's arms so that it gently touches the bottom of his chin.

"Good to see you again chief," says Raid. "We thought this volcano town you kept talking about sounded like fun so we drove up here with the girls and here you are."

"Do you like our new machetes?" asks Tron, who towers over Garcia by half a foot. "We liked your friend's so much we decided to get our own."

"I don't know who you are or what you think you're doing," says Snow, "but this situation has nothing to do with you."

"Anyway," says Raid, not paying attention to Snow, "we saw your son over there with that stranger so we got worried. And then we remembered your story about some crazy sea captain and we see this fellow here in his little boating hat and thought we should say hello."

"Yes, we thought saying hello would be the right thing to do," says Tron.

"And the girls wanted to say hi, too," says Raid. "Say hi girls!"

Snow and I turn our heads to see the two call girls at my son's table. Lopez nowhere to be seen. The girls smile, waving back, playfully mussing my son's hair.

"Saying hello was the right thing to do," I say, taking a sip of my drink.

"We'd very much like to take your captain friend on a hike," says Raid.

"Yes," says Tron. "We're hiking around the volcanoes and would like him to come along."

"It's very steep though," says Raid.

"Very steep indeed," says Tron.

"We'll have to watch our step," says Raid.

"Most definitely some tricky parts here and there," says Tron.

Snow is suddenly speechless. Raid tells him to hand me his pistol, which he does almost matter-of-factly.

I tell Garcia to get up from the bar and calmly go back to his village, which he does. Then I tell Raid I need to do something before taking my son to see Haas and if the girls can watch him while they go on their "hike."

"Of course," says Raid. "The girls love your little boy."

"It's good to see you," I say.

"It's good to see you, too," he says looking around as he finishes off his cognac. "It's not so big a country you know. Norway is much bigger than this place."

"I must visit sometime," I say.

"Yes, you'll have to meet our wives and go fishing for brown trout. You and your son."

The Nords leave with Captain Snow, and my son and I have dinner in the lobby with the hookers. We eat BLTs together, exhausted and smiling, volcanoes looming up in the big windows behind us.

VOLCÁN DE AMERICANO

EVEN THOUGH IT'S Italian, my Beretta is the most American thing I own. More American than blue jeans or living inside a Sitka Spruce with your son, eating squirrel meat.

Beretta was founded in the 16ᵗʰ century. Not long after the Spanish set up camp in Florida, looking for the fountain of youth.

Originally, I wanted to get the M1951 "Egyptian" model, which was more of a deep Lake Tahoe blue, but SFPD gave everyone the same standard issue black M9. Not that I liked shooting at people. Maybe just the idea of guns intrigued me in some way.

It's early in the morning now.

I'm sitting on the edge of the bed, kissing my sleeping son on the forehead.

I lay the M9 and Snow's Sig Sauer into a paper bag like steel ingots of death. I take some chips and a beer from the mini-bar and lay those on top of the guns.

I take a taxi to the police station. I roll down the window. Smells of strong coffee, bread, and quartz percolate through the cab.

Once at the station, I go to the front desk and ask to see the officers who saved the American the other day on the volcano.

A few minutes later another officer appears and asks what I want.

I tell him I'm a police chief from the United States on vacation and would like the honor of a ride-along with the brave officers that saved the American woman. I show him my badge and tell him I even brought my own lunch, waving my paper bag in his face.

He says they don't really do ride-alongs down here, but I can tell he's intrigued by the idea of a police chief from the old U.S. of A. wanting to see some of his officers in action.

He asks if I will pose for a photograph.

"Of course," I say.

I hold my badge up while someone at the front desk takes a picture of us.

"I like you American cops," says the officer. "What city are you in?"

I tell him an island in the far north, but that I used to be a cop in San Francisco.

"Ah, San Francisco," he says excitedly. "The Dirty Harry!"

Then he tells me to wait there.

Ten minutes later two other officers descend the stairs. They have on black tactical gear and dark blue ball caps that say "Policía."

Their names are Reyes and Perez. They aren't very talkative but admit they're the ones who escorted the American and the Japanese up the volcano.

"You must be very brave," I tell them.

Reyes smiles a polite thank you, but the other one, Perez, won't even look in my direction. He says something quickly in Spanish that makes Reyes' smile disappear.

We leave the station through downtown out past the outer ring of hotels and motels, then muddy fields and farms, finally out near the highway where a stroke of thick green canopy chokes either side.

Knowing I don't have long, I ask if we can pull over for lunch somewhere. Reyes lets out a bored sigh and stops at a roadside sandwich cart.

Just as they're about to open their doors I open my bag and take out the two pistols, putting one to each of the backs of their heads.

"Donde esta el dinero?" I ask them in fly-by-night Spanish.

"What kind of gringo cop are you?" yells Reyes.

I ask him about the money again.

They both look straight ahead, saying nothing, so I shoot Reyes in the foot. When he bends screaming to look at the new hole in his boot, I rap him on the back of the head with the Sig. I tell him to sit straight or he loses another toe.

Reyes sits straight.

"My boy is dying," I tell them. "You will die too if you don't tell me where the American woman's money is."

Reyes says something in Spanish.

"His foot," says Perez. "He can't drive with the foot."

I nod and Perez switches places with him in the driver's seat like he was a concerned designated driver from our sister sorority.

Then they drive me through a papaya grove away from the highway. We climb a steep hill into a mist before we arrive at a lake. It is a very small lake, almost more of a bog really. As if dinosaurs were still living there, hiding somewhere in the soupy gray haze.

At the northern tip of the lake there is an old RV resting at the edge of the jungle like a sleeping triceratops.

We get out and Reyes knocks on the door of the RV. Four other policemen drunkenly pile out. There are two girls with them in their underwear. One of the officers is shirtless, his nipples distractingly large for a man of his size. For a brief moment, they stand there looking at me. Volcanoes behind them. Pterodactyl bones. Papaya flash in the distance like dim orange streetlamps of 1950s London.

It takes the drunk officers a few seconds to realize this isn't a joke. When they realize it isn't a joke, they get a look on their faces like maybe it'd be a good idea to bum rush me.

While keeping one gun trained on them, I point the other gun at their RV and empty half the clip, shooting out a few windows and a tire. They have a different look on their faces now. A look that says, *lo conseguimos loco joder.*

"Which one of you stabbed the American woman?" I ask, pointing both guns at them again.

Three of the officers take a step back, leaving just the shirtless man with the nipples.

Nipples-man smiles at me.

He is armed with the easy confidence of a tangential bible character who never should've made it past Leviticus. "Escucha, amigo, pero…"

Before he can finish, I shoot him in the foot, sending him to the ground, screaming.

"Why you keep shooting everyone in the foot!" yells Perez.

I tell the girls to find their clothes and get in the back of the car. I then have all the officers line up and put handcuffs on the officer next to them. After that I tell them to sit down. Then I have Reyes, whose boot is pretty well soaked with blood by now, to point out where the money is.

He nods to the engine.

I lift the hood and find Katherine's backpack just sitting there next to the carburetor. Captain Snow was right after all. Some things are easy.

I take all their tactical belts and throw them in the lake. I put on Reyes' blue "Policía" cap and mirrored sunglasses. I suddenly feel more American than apple pie, or sunshine acid from the dark web.

"How do I look?" I ask him, sticking a gun up his left nostril.

Driving back, I miraculously find a radio station playing Steely Dan. Who in Guatemala is listening to Steely Dan, I think. I turn it up as I drive past papaya streetlamps and ghosts of the Jurassic at eighty miles an hour, smoking a cigarette I asked one of the girls for. We don't talk the whole way, the sounds of turbulence and fluegelhorn filling the police car.

I let the them off on the outskirts of town.

They are trying to hold back tears.

"Remember me," I tell the girls as I drive away. "Yo soy el Volcan de Americano!"

BANANA PUDDING

KATHERINE'S LAST DAY at the hospital is sunny and warm with high blue skies. No one was expecting it to be her last day, but what do hospitals know? Before I see her, I pack our stuff and settle the hotel bill. Then I go to the safe to get Katherine's backpack of money and ours. Then I say goodbye to the Pooles. I want to say goodbye to Raid and Tron, but the call girls say they're still on their "hiking trip" with Captain Snow and might not be back till tomorrow.

I take some hotel stationary and write down my address on Wolf Island and under that I write, *If you ever want to fly fish the Great Pacific NW and discuss the finer points of milk vs. cognac... I owe you one. Adios, Chief Bell.*

I give the note to the call girls.

"Gracias," I tell them. And I give them both a hug, their fake boobs squeezing out to the sides like trapped hot air balloons.

My son and I have a big beautiful breakfast of eggs and bacon with croissants and butter in a café across the street. Then we go out and buy some fresh flowers from a stand. After that we casually walk around a little because we're still early for visiting hours. We amble along a town square with some trees and a little bandstand for festivals. The cobblestone streets come alive with bus stop debates and mopeds carrying short-skirted women and crates stuffed with multi-colored chickens. When the church bell rings for nine o'clock we go inside. We walk up to the second floor and see a whirl of doctors and nurses at the end of the hall.

What's all the commotion, I wonder? I walk carefully down the hall as if my legs know something I don't. I tell my son to wait there, and keep walking as if pulled by some invisible tractor beam meant only for the ex-police chief of Wolf Island.

When the tractor beam is done with me, I am standing outside Katherine's room.

"You can't be here right now," a nurse says to me.

"But I know her," I say.

"She's going into surgery right now. Please wait in the lobby and we'll find you after."

I try to get a good look at Katherine through all the doctors and the machines, but it's impossible, so my son and I head to the lobby. He rubs one of his eyes.

"How're your eyes, champ?" I ask.

"Good," he says, and he stops rubbing it.

My son asks me if I miss home.

I tell him I do, but that I like the adventure we're on together, too.

"Do you think mom likes a-ventures?" he asks.

"Of course," I say, trying not to think about what they're doing to Katherine right now. "It's just that this adventure is only for you and me."

My son squints at me the way he does when he's not so sure about the information he's just been given.

"Remember that race car video game at the arcade?" I ask.

"By the beach?"

"That's the one. Well, that race car could only hold one adult and one kid and that's sort of like the adventure we're on. There's only so much room."

"But Marty isn't on the a-venture anymore."

"Well, he sort of is. He's just not with us right now."

"Do you think there will be a-ventures just me and mom go on?"

"Sure."

"Will you feel bad?"

"About what, son?"

"About not being on the a-venture with us?"

"A little, yeah. But I can always just wait my turn for the next adventure, right?"

"Are we going to see mom soon?"

"You bet. Just a few more days and then we'll fly home."

My son sighs deeply like this had all really been weighing on him. I smile at him and he smiles back.

It isn't long after that when a doctor and nurse arrive to tell me that Katherine is dead.

He says "internal bleeding" with great solemnity, as if Moses himself had taken those words down from the mount like stone tablets and rolled them down the hospital hallway, breaking everyone's heart.

For a long time, I don't say anything.

I just sort of sit down thinking about her gobs of Burmese jade, and shock of white hair, and mediocre huckleberry jam. I'm thinking about this while looking somewhere over my son's head. There's nothing there, of course, except a newspaper stand and an old shoeshine box, but I look there anyway because my eyes don't know where else to go.

I don't lie down on the floor.

I don't start smooshing avocados into my mouth.

I don't take out the Beretta and shoot myself in the foot.

I don't even decide to become a bartender in a remote mountain town that only gets mild foot-traffic during ski season and the rest of the year you hike up to glacier melt ponds to find some old Piper Cub wreckage from the 70s, then when you find it, take your shirt off and drink a beer and eat Cool Ranch Doritos, feeling good to be alive, and not pulverized against the rocks of some dormant volcano.

"What about her son?" I ask.

"We most likely will put a shunt in tomorrow morning. It's too bad, but it will be better for him. His father is arriving on a flight this evening."

I hand the doctor Katherine's backpack.

"Please give this to him. My son and I have to leave town, but this was Katherine's so he should have it."

The doctor thanks me and they turn to walk away.

"Did she say anything?" I ask.

The doctor turns, "Que? Sorry, what was that?"

"Was there anything she said at the end?" I ask.

"She's been unconscious since this morning, sir."

"What about last night? Did she say anything before she went to sleep?"

"I don't know," the doctor says. "Unfortunately, I was off until this morning..."

The nurse suddenly takes a step forward into the conversation, "Banana pudding," she says to me.

"Excuse me?" I say.

"She asked for seconds of the banana pudding," says the nurse. "She liked it very, very much. She always eat it both nights. Those were her last words. Then she...she go to sleep."

"Banana pudding," I say.

"Banana pudding," says the nurse.

"I'm sorry for your loss," says the doctor.

PLACE OF FLOWERS

VOLCÁN DE AGUA, also known by the Mayans as Hunahpu, or "place of flowers," is a stratovolcano that towers 12,340 feet above the Pacific coastal plain to the south and the Guatemalan Central Highlands to the north.

The volcano dwarfs the nearby landscape like the beginning of a big-budget disaster movie.

Volcán de Agua is popular with coffee growers on its lower slopes and above the cloud line is often frequented by fathers and their sons whose brains are trying to kill them.

If your son was dying, you would go there, too.

The only other places you would go are 99th and Madison, or your water-logged backyard to crawl into the bushes and never come out again.

But those places are hopeless.

Those places have nothing to look forward to except for barberry stickers and squirrels, the smell of heated canned corn, and people who haven't showered in three days, weeping next to vending machines.

Volcanoes look out at the world in every direction as if saying "hello" to everyone at once. Volcanoes are like the host who spins in the front hall with the overcoats and a bottle of bubbly. They're quite welcoming for something that has the potential to fry off your face like Fontina.

It's good to remember the best time of year to ascend the volcano is whenever you're there.

Lava doesn't care about things like seasons.

Jaguars, monks, your friends and relatives. None of them give a shit either. They have their own lives and your tragedy is just a random news bulletin to ruin their breakfast, or trip to Disneyland.

You and the volcano are on your own.

You will be the only one to see his little socks for the last time.

You will be the only one that decides what song should potentially be the last one he ever hears.

Volcán de Agua is where we are now.

It took our entire lives to get to this volcano overlooking Guatemala and the Mariana Trench and my dad's beer bottle from 1984. Everywhere you go it takes your entire life to get there, except I'm pretty sure this place is different. It's not like

Wolf Island or 99th and Madison. This place has answers, which can be extremely rare and silvery colored with a high melting point. They are more valuable than rhodium or the red diamond.

My son and I pass by a river and a lake on our way to the volcano's northern apron, spreading out black and green like the great bruised pyramid of Giza. It's a beautiful volcano. We're walking towards the clouds. Haas has got to be up there somewhere, I think.

"When will we get there?" asks my son.

"Probably just before bedtime," I tell him, feeling the Beretta and the Sig Sauer and the twenty-five thousand dollars shifting in my pack.

"Can I throw some rocks in there," he says, pointing to the lake.

"Just a few," I say. "Then we have to keep moving."

My son has a good arm. Throws rocks like Roberto Clemente. Together we watch the water go "sploosh," then wait for another.

I think about Dr. Haas. What will I say when I see him? "Here he is?" "Let's get down to brass tacks?" "Hi there?"

I think about Katherine.

I think about Marty.

I think about the Pacific.

I miss the way water has a purpose in the ocean. A deeper sort of meaning and overall sense of direction. Lake water is something different altogether. It is, for lack of a better word, directionless. That's because lakes are shallow and emotionally cut off from the world. Rivers, of course, are a little better, but they're always in a rush to get somewhere, and what good is life without taking a breather here and there?

One day we'll go back to the Pacific.

We'll watch the churning blue-green with sandwiches and beer. Maybe my future ex-wife will leave the desert and join us every once in a while. Civility in the face of so much unrest. I don't think it's a stretch to say that people who visit the ocean on a regular basis have a certain perspective on things. They watch the waves, and the sky, and the birds, and that cacophony of color and sound tells you something about yourself if you let it.

"How about it?" I say to my son who throws one more rock.

"Sploosh!" says the rock.

ACKNOWLEDGEMENTS

Thanks to Andy Babbitz, Samuel Douglas, Daniel Menaker and everyone at Unsolicited Press for making this a better book.

A tip of the cap to Richard Brautigan, Donald Barthelme, Kate Jennings and Sufjan Stevens.

And to the folks who got me here: Meredith Hays, Thomas Beller, Larry Colton, Margo Wilding, Michael Benware, the old crew at Little, Brown and the San Telmo Round Table.

Of course, mom and dad.

To Dr. Berenstein, who saved our little boy.

And to Jules, the fearless one.

Lucy and Ford, you are in my dreams.

ABOUT THE AUTHOR

Trevor J. Houser lives with his family in Seattle. He has published stories in *Zyzzyva*, *Story Quarterly* and *The Doctor TJ Eckleburg Review* among others. Three of his stories were nominated for the Pushcart Prize.

ABOUT THE PRESS

Unsolicited Press was founded in 2012 and is based in Portland, Oregon. The small press publishes fiction, poetry, and creative nonfiction written by award-winning and emerging authors. Some of its authors include John W. Bateman, Anne Leigh Parrish, Adrian Ernesto Cepeda, and Raki Kopernik.

Learn more at www.unsolicitedpress.com

CPSIA information can be obtained
at www.ICGtesting.com
Printed in the USA
FSHW010057011221
86460FS